TO DIE IN DINETAH

THE DARK LEGACY OF KIT CARSON

JOHN A. TRUETT

SUNSTONE PRESS

SANTA FE
NEW MEXICO

My deepest thanks to Roy L. Jones
who, so many times, kept me from
falling out of the saddle during that
agonizing ride up a mountain trail
that always looked impossible.

© 1994 by John A. Truett

All Rights Reserved

This novel, although suggested by events in the life of Kit Carson, has been fictionalized and contains characters and incidents created for dramatic purposes.

First edition

Printed in the United States of America

Library of Congress Cataloging in Publication Data

Truett, John A., 1927
      To die in Dinetah : the dark legacy of Kit Carson   / John A. Truett.
-- 1st ed.
         p. cm.
      ISBN 0-86534-225-3 : $14.95
      1. Carson, Kit, 1809-1868--Fiction. 2. Frontier and pioneer life--west (U.S.)--
Fiction. 3. Scouts and scouting--West (U.S.)--Fiction. 4. Navajo Indians--
Relocation--Fiction. 5. Pioneers--West (U.S.)--Fiction. 6. Soldiers--West
(U.S.)--Fiction. 7. Navajo Indians--Wars--Fiction.   I. Title.
      PS3570.R813T6   1994
      813' .54--dc20
                                                                94-12376
                                                                CIP

Published by Sunstone Press
                    Post Office Box 2321
                    Santa Fe, New Mexico 87504-2321 / USA
                    (505) 988-4418 / FAX: (505) 988-1025
                    orders only (800) 243-5644

PROLOGUE

Captain Nicholas Hodt frowned as he sniffed the tension-filled air. It had the same smell of a dry desert storm, moving ominously across the New Mexico land in ugly gray-black clouds, threatening to hurtle down bolts of jagged white lightning.

The soldiers at Fort Fauntleroy were restless, Indians weren't raising hell any more, war had broken out in the east and the prospect of battle was like a pestering chigger. The men were itching to fight.

It made the hair on Nicholas Hodt's arms bristle as he walked past the enlisted men's quarters and he took a deep breath to clear his mind. Unable to shake the edgy feeling, he went to the fort's gates to watch crowds of Navajos arriving in the warm sun to receive their monthly rations.

The Indians accepted their food with grunts of thanks and then began trading among the soldiers—blankets and trinkets for whiskey. Hodt's eyes squinted in disapproval. Giving liquor to the Indians was like pulling whiskers on a wildcat's cheeks, but he had nothing to say in the matter; the officer in charge condoned it.

Although whiskey flowed on both sides, things seemed to be going peacefully. Until late afternoon. During the horse races between Indians and enlisted men, reins of a Navajo pony were secretly cut and the race was lost. A loud protest sprang from the outraged Indians with one of them demanding a new race, but he was answered by the roar of a gun—a drunken soldier pulled his weapon and shot down the old Navajo in cold blood.

Like a match in a powder keg, Fort Fauntleroy exploded. Whiskey-inflamed soldiers grabbed their guns and the Indians fled, screaming in terror as soldiers gave chase with shouting and gunfire. The commanding officer was quick to order a howitzer trained on the helpless victims.

Captain Hodt rushed out amid the bedlam to stop the massacre, but the men seemed to have gone mad as they shot, clubbed and stabbed the Indians.

A soldier plunged his bayonet into the back of a squaw who was running with two small children in her arms and Hodt ran up as the woman fell screaming to the ground.

"Stop it there, soldier!" Hodt yelled.

The man gave him only a glance and shoved his bayonet into the stomach of one child, then smashed both their heads with the butt of his rifle.

"You're under arrest!" Hodt cried and grabbed the soldier's gun.

A lieutenant rushed over with his pistol drawn at full cock. "Give back that soldier's weapon," he demanded, "or else I'll shoot you, God damn you!"

The captain had no other choice. He returned the soldier's rifle and looked helplessly at the dozens of sprawled Indians, killed by cannon, gunshot and bayonet. He knew that word of the massacre would spread quickly and the Indians would only go back to their raiding and killing of innocent settlers.

The whole senseless thing made Nicholas Hodt's gut wrench, for today's violence had destroyed all the work Colonel Canby had done to achieve peace with the Indians. But the colonel could wash his hands of the affair—he was being sent back east to fight in the war and it was now up to his replacement, General James Carleton, as Commander of the New Mexico Department.

Captain Nicholas Hodt shrugged in defeat. He wondered what General Carleton, a hundred miles to the north at Santa Fe, would do, now, to stop the carnage that lay ahead.

◆◆◆

The capital city was bustling with wagons and carts full of produce clattering through the square when Kit Carson rode into Santa Fe. The famous Indian fighter, still agile at fifty-two with broad shoulders and auburn hair flowing down the back of his neck, was dressed in his usual buckskin pants and shirt.

Carson pondered the reason why General Carleton had asked him to come to the capital for a conference, but it would be good to see his old friend again; together, they had fought the Jicarilla Apaches years earlier when Carleton arrived in the Territory with his California Column.

James H. Carleton considered himself a Christian humanitarian and Kit Carson admired the man. However, the soldiers serving under Carleton thought otherwise. To them, James Carleton was arbitrary and sometimes cruel; he was unscrupulous, ambitious and selfish. With his aggressive, strong chin, dark piercing eyes, flowing sideburns and a thick heavy moustache, he radiated a tyrannical personality.

Now, James Carleton was all smiles as Kit Carson came into the Palace of

Governors office with his familiar slight stoop. The general grasped Carson's hand warmly. "Kit! I'm pleased to see you again—it's been too long!"

"And good to see you, General." Kit Carson's blue-gray eyes still held their serious penetrating look above a drooping reddish moustache as he seated himself in front of the general's large desk.

"The reason I asked you here," Carleton said, "is because something has to be done about the raiding and killing by Indians in the Territory. I'm planning a war against them to bring this to a stop, and I couldn't think of any other man than you to help me do the job! What do you say, Kit?"

Carleton was patient. He knew that when Kit Carson found himself in a serious conversation, his reply was slow and deliberate, sometimes with a pause while searching for the exact word. After a moment's thought, Carson spoke.

"I've lived with the Indians and speak most o' their tongue. The only reason they're raidin' and killin' is because the Mexicans and Anglos here have done the same thing t'them. . .even takin' their children to sell as slaves." He trained experienced eyes on the general. "I think the Indians would come to terms without a war."

"But my predecessor Colonel Canby tried that and it didn't work. The Indians broke their treaty with him and started marauding again."

Carson knew why—the senseless killing of the Navajo men, women and children at Fort Fauntleroy. But he kept his silence and let the general continue.

"I've asked Governor Connelly to have Washington bring us more soldiers into New Mexico. With the additional troops, I want to fulfill Colonel Canby's grand idea of forcing the Indians to surrender and putting them on a reservation."

Carson chuckled at the thought. "That's a mighty grand idea, all right!"

"But it's one that I know will work, and only you can help me do it!" The general eased into cajoling familiarity. "Kit, you're still a colonel in charge of the First New Mexico Volunteers. I know that you are devoutly loyal to your country and to the men who are running it. You're the only man capable of working with the Indians to bring about peace and you'll be demonstrating that loyalty if you cooperate with me in this matter."

Carson warmed to the flattery. He was also restless after quitting his job running the Ute Indian Agency and the thought of getting back into action was tempting. "And jest how d'you want me to cooperate?"

"First, I want you to round up your Volunteers again and reoccupy Fort Stanton in Apache country. Let me know when you've got it running and

I'll send you further orders."

Kit Carson gave it a long moment of consideration before replying.

"I don't like the idea of gittin' into another war, but if we can git the Indians to live in peace on a reservation, I reckon it'd be worth a try."

After Kit Carson left, General Carleton was filled with self-satisfaction and went immediately to Governor Connelly's office with the news.

"Carson jumped at the opportunity to help his country. He's agreed to help me fight the Indians, and after he's settled at Fort Stanton, I'll give him orders to start killing off the Apaches first! By then, he'll be in so deep, he'll have to do as I say or else feel he's betraying his country."

The governor was pleased at the cunning way General Carleton had drawn Kit Carson into the plan.

"That's good!" Connelly said with an eager smile. "New troops should be arriving in another few weeks—I'm just as keen as you to get this thing under way!"

CHAPTER ONE

Terry O'Neill found the recruitment depot at David's Island in New York to be what he'd expected—a hell hole. Along with the other recruits, he was issued ill-fitting clothing, which included heavy neck-to-ankle underwear that itched like the devil in the warm weather, and rough boots that quickly wore a blister on his feet.

If the clothes were unsuitable, the food was even worse. For breakfast there was coffee, sometimes with no cream or sugar, salt pork and either fried mush or a thin stew that had cooked all night. At noon came more dry bread, coffee and, with any luck, three prunes.

After two weeks of marching, exercises and fatigue detail, Terry laid his aching body down on the hard straw mattress and dreamed of the wonderful meals his mother cooked at their Monmouth home in the Catskills; or the elegant dinners at the house of his fiance's parents in New York City, all served on a linen tablecloth with utensils of sterling silver.

His daydreaming was interrupted by Ben Adams who came into the barracks, red hair waving like the small flames of a campfire. It was unusual to see excitement in Ben's eyes, for he had always been the quiet farm boy.

Ben took a deep breath. "There's an Indian uprisin' in New Mexico, and they're askin' for volunteers to be assigned to a fort there—what do you say we go, Terry?"

"But we joined up to fight the Confederates here—why should we go all the way out west and shoot Indians?"

"Well, you know I don't like the idea of havin' to shoot anybody in this war. I figured as long as I gotta serve my country, I wouldn't mind so much if it was just an Indian I had to kill."

That was one thing Terry couldn't understand about Ben. Working on a farm, it must have been an everyday event, slaughtering hogs, wringing chicken necks, even shooting a cow so stuck in mud it couldn't be pulled out. But it bothered Ben Adams to have to kill anything.

Terry had met him right after Ben came to New York to get away from the hard farm life. Ben got a job as groom at the stables in a New York Park where Terry liked to ride horses in his spare time and the two became fast friends. Ben enjoyed working with animals and was happy at his job, until that day at the stables when he had to kill a horse. Ben's face was like a deflated balloon when Terry arrived for his usual ride.

"Looks like you just lost a good friend," Terry said with amusement.

Ben ran a shaking hand through his carrot-red hair. "It's Rusty Rose. Hasn't been able to get up ever since she stepped into that hole this week. The leg's broken—you know what that means!"

Ben and Terry both loved Rusty Rose and Terry always rented out the gentle mare whenever she was available.

"Rusty Rose?!" Terry answered. "There must be a way to save her!"

"Two docs have examined her and said there wasn't any hope she'd walk again." Ben held up a small black box. "I got the stable owner's gun here, but. . ." He held back a sob. "I just cain't do it, Terry!"

Terry was saddened, too, but he was also practical. "Ben, she can't just lie on her side the rest of her life!"

Ben shook his head and Terry knew they had a problem. He took the box from Ben's hand. "If you want me to, I'll do it for you."

Ben looked up in shock. "You mean you can go in there and shoot her?! A horse you rode all the time and liked more than any of the other ones?"

"Ben, I know how you feel about Rusty Rose, and I love her, too. But it's something that has to be done—and it won't hurt me as much as it would you."

Ben sat down on a hitching rail and Terry took the gun into the stables. It was difficult, looking at the stricken animal lying on a pallet of straw, its pained eyes pleading for help, but Terry stroked her mane and laid the pistol barrel against its head. He hoped Ben would understand and forgive him.

It had been no problem with Terry. He and his father often shot down quail, rabbits and deer with their guns in the mountains behind their house in the Catskills. Even when he joined the Army, he thought that when the time came, killing a man wouldn't be much different.

Now, as Ben stood in the recruitment barracks, waiting for a reply to his suggestion of going west, Terry was intrigued.

"Maybe you're right," he said. "Taking aim on a line of Indians would be like one of those carnival shooting galleries. Besides, with the white man claiming the west, Indians need to be taken care of, anyway!"

Terry left the comfort of his hard straw cot and went with Ben to the headquarters building where they signed the volunteer list. Terry clapped a hand on Ben's shoulder.

"Well, Ben, if this doesn't work out, I'll have only you to blame!"

Ben's face glowed with relief. "It'll work out, don't you worry none. I feel better already!"

Early the following morning, Terry and Ben joined a small group of other volunteers with packs and rifles on their backs to be herded by a growling Sergeant Baines onto a train in New York. Baines had a bulldog voice with temperament to match, and the men were discouraged to learn that the sergeant, who had served in New Mexico before, would be going west with them.

"Settle down," Baines told the men. "You got a long trip ahead of you. Soon's we reach the rail terminal at Cheyenne, you'll go by wagon to your assignment."

The sergeant wasn't joking. At first, it was slow and boring, with a change of trains and many stops to discharge and take on passengers, but the train eventually puffed its way out onto the plains where distant hills glistened with undulating grass. Ben slumped half asleep, hair moving like a red feather over his nose as he breathed, while Terry sat next to him, gazing out the window. The clack-clacking sound of the train and restful countryside moving past him eased Terry's thoughts gently back to all those he'd left behind in New York.

Saying goodbye to his parents was bad enough, but the worst thing about joining the Army was having to quit his job at Carper's Weekly. The publisher, Sam Godfrey, and his wife hated to see Terry go. The Godfreys loved Terry as much as their daughter Susan, whom he was to marry, and it got so that Terry ate most of his meals at the Godfrey home.

Sam Godfrey assured Terry that his writing job would be waiting when he got back from the war, then Terry went to the riding stables to tell Susan the sad news. As long as he lived, the smell of horses would conjure up the lovely face of Susan Godfrey, for she and Terry both loved horses and had met at the stables.

He found Susan on a favorite white horse, her blonde hair tastefully pinned up beneath a little feathered hat and a bright red coat protecting her slim body from the cold breeze. A crisp long skirt covered her legs as she sat erect in the sidesaddle, a leather crop in hand. With the dark green trees as a background, Susan Godfrey reminded Terry of one of those old-master paintings he'd seen in the museum.

"Terry!" she cried with delight.

He walked over to help her down and she slid into his arms. They kissed shamelessly in front of Ben Adams who grinned and began removing the saddle from her horse.

"Why aren't you at the office?" she asked as Terry released her. "Did Daddy give you the afternoon off?"

"Yes, for the next three years."

"What are you talking about—he didn't fire you, did he?"

"No, I quit!"

"Oh, Terry, stop teasing. What happened?"

"I decided to join the Army, after all. In fact, I just came from the recruiting office."

She was aghast. "You're in the Army? But Daddy said he could get you out of conscription!"

"I had to do it, Susan—I want to fight for my country, like all the others."

"And what about our marriage?"

He put an arm around her small waist. "We'll have to wait till I get back. It's only three years."

"Three years? Terry, I love you—I don't want to wait three years!"

She had cried when he pulled her close and the warm tears on his shirt made him feel maybe he'd done the wrong thing.

Now, the clackity-clack rhythm began to slow and the train finally chugged to a stop. Jets of steam gushing from the boilers roused Ben who sat up with expectation. "Are we there already?"

Terry opened the window to peer ahead with astonishment. "Ben, come look at this!"

Ben stuck his head out the window and they watched as a tremendous herd of buffalo surrounded the train's engine. The huge beasts were crossing the tracks, in their own good time, while moving south to feed on new grass. The engineer blew the whistle again and again, but to no avail.

The pullman came to life with all the soldiers hanging out of windows to view the spectacle. One of them was Grizzly Taylor, a burly man with a dark beard who had been a menace to everyone at David's Island. He grabbed his gun and pushed it through the window next to Terry.

"Gonna git me a buffalo!" Grizzly said as he took aim.

Terry's finger itched. He'd never shot anything that large. He, too, grabbed his rifle and poked it out of the window.

The docile animals milled around the train like sitting ducks, oblivious to man's intrusion on their God-given land. Grizzly fired twice, but no buffalo dropped to the ground. He uttered a curse. "The hide on them damned animals must be a foot thick!"

Terry realized any animal that big and tough had to be killed a certain way. He aimed for a buffalo's eye and fired. The scruffy beast whirled around, then fell to its knees and rolled over.

Grizzly gave him a sour look. "Where'd you learn to shoot like that?"

"My father taught me," Terry said proudly. "He owns a gun shop back home."

There were shouts of excitement from the other men as they also fired through the windows, until Sergeant Baines came roaring through the car. "Put them guns away! There's no shootin' allowed from the train. Save your ammunition for when you need it!"

Scraggly manes of the large dark-brown animals swept the ground as they finally stomped over the tracks and drifted across the prairie in a thundering cloud of dust.

When the train lumbered like a tired dying monster into the rail terminal at Cheyenne, it was early morning and Sergeant Baines walked through the car, waking each soldier with a punch in the back.

"Rise and shine!" he roared. "You've had it easy so far. Now, get your gear together. . .we'll be takin' a wagon from here to New Mexico."

Several wagons stood waiting, pulled by mules and driven by Army men. Sergeant Baines sat up front with one of the drivers while the soldiers crowded together in the wagons with little room to move a leg. They traveled south under a hot sun, stopping to rest at noon, and then continued until sundown, to eat a meager supper and sleep under the open skies. Two soldiers were always posted every two hours for guard duty, in case of Indians. However, no redskins were seen.

The tired group finally arrived in Santa Fe, New Mexico, where more wagons stood with gruff-looking sergeants holding the reins. The sixty men were divided into groups of ten to be taken to various outlying forts in the Territory; Terry and Ben were among those going to Fort Stanton with Sergeant Baines.

"Grab your guns and get that equipment on your backs," Baines ordered. "Let's get a move on!"

The men strapped on their heavy packs, took their rifles and walked over to the new wagon but saw that it was full of supplies.

Ben Adams turned to Sergeant Baines. "Where's the wagon we're to ride in?"

The sergeant gave a hearty laugh. "Ride?! You're gonna walk to Fort Stanton, soldier!"

"Walk?! Just how far is it?"

"Oh, I'd say 'bout a hundred and fifty miles." Baines climbed up onto the seat next to the other sergeant who would be driving the two mules. "Just walk in double file behind us and keep up, or we'll leave you here on the desert for the coyotes to chew on!"

Again, the sergeant wasn't joking and the ten soldiers began trudging behind the wagon as it started off across the prairie. The sun rose with malicious glee, soaking the men with perspiration, while dust from the wagon flew back, turning to mud on their faces. The heavy pack straps rubbed their skin raw as Terry and Ben stumbled at the rear of the suffering line, wiping stinging sweat out of their eyes.

It finally became too much for Ben. "Dadburn!" he said. "I got a blister on my heel big as one of them mules!"

Terry wanted to laugh but his throat was too dry. "Don't forget, Ben, this was all your idea!"

"I'd take my shoes off, but this sand's hotter'n my Ma's iron stove on bread-makin' day!" Ben limped along, trying to keep up.

Finally, at noon, the wagon stopped and the men dropped to the ground, sprawling like dehydrated corpses on the sand. They drank eagerly from their canteens, even though the water was hot.

"We'll take a nooner here till the sun starts goin' down," Sergeant Baines said and walked over to a couple of steaming bodies. He kicked each with his boot. "You and you—take the first guard duty. And remember, if you see any sign of Indians, give a yell!"

Baines and the other sergeant sat in the wagon seat, leaning back with their hats pulled down over their eyes and a shotgun propped between their legs.

The recruits lay half asleep in the hot sun with hats over their faces, each one praying he wouldn't be picked as the next replacement guards.

Ben had taken off his shoe and sock to ease the raw blister. "If any Indians do show up," he muttered, "just let 'em put an arrow in me. I'd be better off than this!"

Soon the heat ebbed and they started out again, forcing themselves over the hard dry prairie. Toward day's end, Terry was staggering almost in delirium, the soles of his feet burning through the scuffed shoe leather, and he fought to keep his head up. The wagon finally stopped and everyone collapsed.

Two soldiers, scrawny Deacon Jones and his sad-looking buddy Moony Calhoun, retrieved some dry bushes to make a fire and everyone sat around the meager flames, somberly waiting for the coffee to boil.

"I shore am gettin' tired of bacon an' hardtack ever' meal!" the man named Al Simmons complained.

"What you expect in the Army, pheasant under glass?" Grizzly Taylor laughed.

"Anything different would be good!" Simmons replied. Then he noticed a movement beneath the wagon and grinned. "Maybe I will have somethin' different." He lifted his rifle, took careful aim and fired toward the wagon. The men jumped at the blast.

"What the hell you shootin' at?!" Sergeant Baines yelled.

Al Simmons walked over to the wagon and bent down. He pulled out a long dead rattlesnake by the tail. "My supper!" he replied.

They all watched as Al Simmons took a knife and carefully skinned the snake, then cut the raw flesh into pieces. He threaded the meat onto a stick and held it over the fire. A few minutes later everyone ate their tasteless supper while Simmons eagerly devoured his gourmet meal of snake meat.

"We're gonna call you Snake Eater Simmons!" Grizzly Taylor said with contempt.

Moony Calhoun shoveled in the beans from a tin plate and said with a mouth full, "Hey, Sarge, think we might see some Indians? Everybody keeps talkin' about 'em, but we ain't seen any yet."

"Don't git too eager," Baines grumbled. "You'll see 'em. They're all around. You'll be lucky at Fort Stanton, though—that's Apache territory and there ain't as many of 'em. But where we are, now, it's Navajo land. Thousands of 'em, and you guards keep yer eyes open tonight!" He took his empty tin plate and cleaned it with sand. "Now finish up and hit your blankets. We're startin' out early in the mornin' and I wanna see all you peckerwoods ready to march at the crack o' dawn!"

When they had rolled up in their blankets that night, Ben couldn't sleep, his mind filled with visions of savage Indians lurking behind every rock. "You reckon it's true what they say about them Indians, Terry?"

Terry was praying for sleep to ease his aching body. "What do they say?"

"That they run a sharp knife around your head and rip off your scalp?"

"You've been reading too many pulp magazines."

"Well, I wonder what they're really like."

"Oh, they probably live in dirty tepees. . .run around naked. . .worship pagan gods. . ."

Terry's voice faded away as he slipped mercifully into sleepy oblivion.

CHAPTER TWO

A crown of snow atop the sacred mountain *Tsoodzil* turned to shining gold under the morning sun as Willow-In-Storm herded her father's sheep onto a small meadow.

The beautiful Navajo girl waited until the animals were content, then sat down to watch the sheep moving like a small white cloud against the distant mountain, their grinding teeth neatly trimming a patch of rich green grass. It was a restful scene and Willow-In-Storm leaned back against the trunk of a large scrub. At quiet moments such as this, she could deal with the troubles in her heart.

She was seventeen years of age and Swift Arrow, one of the young impetuous braves, had announced his plans to steal enough horses to pay for her hand in marriage. This pleased her father very much, but Willow-In-Storm stubbornly rejected the offer. After the white soldiers had killed so many of their people at the fort, Swift Arrow was encouraging the other men to strike back.

"I do not want to marry," Willow-In-Storm told the young brave, "only to find next day that you have been killed in a raid!"

"I will not be killed!" the boy replied. "The medicine man will teach me the Enemy Way ceremony. I will use pollen shaken from a live squirrel and thus be invisible!"

"If that is so, then we will soon have babies, and when they are old enough they will be captured to be sold as slaves!"

"I am strong and will not let our children be taken!"

Willow-In-Storm knew that it would happen anyway and her heart ached for an end to all the fighting. She agreed with her father's brother Standing Bear that if the Diné kept from raiding and killing, maybe the white men would leave them alone to dwell peacefully in Dinetah, the land given to them by the ancient Holy Ones.

If such a thing ever came to pass, then Willow-In-Storm would gladly marry, but it was an unlikely dream. She finally pushed the long raven hair from her shoulders, realizing the sun was low and the sheep had moved too far away; it was time to herd them back home.

When she got to her feet, the tree behind her warmed the air with a soft glow and she turned in awe as the trunk became a shaft of gold light, transforming itself into the form of a beautiful woman. The branches swirled like shining flaxen hair studded with shells and bits of turquoise as Willow-In-Storm stood transfixed by the miraculous image. Then she was aware of a soothing voice. The words came not through her ears but were felt in her heart and she knew it was Changing Woman who spoke.

Long afternoon shadows were stretching through the village when Willow-In-Storm, still tingling from her experience in the meadow, corralled the sheep. She was late in getting back and knew that her father would be waiting impatiently for his meal to be prepared; it was Willow-In-Storm's duty to see to his needs and tend the sheep after her mother's death three years earlier.

"I have seen a strange thing," she told her father as he sat beneath the smoke hole inside their hogan. "Changing Woman appeared to me in the pasture."

Her father looked up in surprise, for Changing Woman was the daughter of First Man and First Woman and one of the most important of Holy People.

"Did Changing Woman speak to you?" he asked.

"Yes, but her words have given me much concern."

The elderly man thought for a moment. "You must say no more to me, for these words should be told to Standing Bear. He is wise and will give you advice."

Her father's brother Standing Bear was an elder *naat' aanii*, or speech maker, and headman of the clan who had many dealings with the white men. He spoke their tongue fluently and taught his niece many of their words.

When Willow-In-Storm entered her uncle's hogan he was sitting at the center fire pit, warming a bowl of food for his evening meal.

"My Father's Brother," she said to him, "I have come to you with a great worry in my heart."

Standing Bear glanced up fondly. "How could such a beautiful girl's heart be plagued with trouble?"

"Changing Woman came to me today while I was herding my father's sheep."

Her uncle's amusement changed to surprise. "Then Changing Woman wishes to bless your marriage to Swift Arrow."

Willow-In-Storm shook her head in irritation. "No, that is not it. She said that Chindi, the god of death, was sitting in his dark cloud, waiting to visit our people."

Standing Bear frowned and stirred his bowl of food. "Perhaps Changing Woman is warning us to take care. I have heard that the good white chief Colonel Canby in Santa Fe, who made peace with the Diné, is being sent back to his people in the east."

Willow-In-Storm trembled. "Then we will have no one to protect us. Surely there will be more killing!"

"They say another man has taken the colonel's place. He is a general with the name of Carleton."

"Does this new one have a heart as big as the one named Canby?"

Standing Bear looked at his niece with uncertain eyes. "We can only wait and see."

CHAPTER THREE

At the first light of dawn, the soldiers started out again on their torturous walk across New Mexico. Terry didn't know if he was getting used to it or if his feet were so numb he couldn't feel the pain.

When the wagon eventually slowed, Terry raised his sweaty eyes in astonishment. The scene ahead was distorted by wavy lines of heat moving across the prairie, but it was real—a small stream surrounded by a few trees.

Sergeant Baines called the group to a halt and announced camp for the night.

"All right, you prairie dogs," he yelled, "you can take a swim in that creek, as long as two guards stand duty!"

Two unhappy soldiers were chosen as guards while the others quickly stripped off their wet sticky clothes and jumped into the stream to roll with ecstasy in the cool water. The two envious guards slumped down with tired sleepy eyes against a tree and waited their turn while Baines and the other sergeant unhitched the mules to feed on patches of grass.

A short distance away, six pairs of Navajo eyes peered through the tree branches. Swift Arrow and his five braves had been on their way to raid a nearby farm when they spotted this wagon trundling across the plain, followed by a group of straggling white soldiers. The Indians couldn't resist; not only were there two mules for the taking, but the wagon was no doubt carrying valuable supplies.

Swift Arrow and his companions felt invincible in their layers of buckskin and with arrows dipped in magic poison made of charcoal from a lightning-struck tree. The hours they had spent in the sweat house, singing and praying to the Wind and Sun People, had given them even more power.

Swift Arrow motioned with his arm for three of his men to attack the soldiers rollicking in the creek while he and the other two braves would surprise the white men unloading the wagon.

While the happy soldiers romped in the water like small boys turned loose to play, the two weary guards rested their aching bodies beneath cool tree branches. It took only a moment for their eyes to close in sleep, unaware of the deadly figures moving toward them through the brush.

"Tell Sarge he can go on without me!" Ben laughed. "I'm gonna stay here!" He gave Terry a playful shove, sending him backward into the stream.

Terry managed to get his head above surface again and rubbed water out of his hair. Suddenly the man behind him cried out in pain and Terry spun around to see the soldier plunge forward with an arrow lodged in his back. The water turned red around Terry's waist and he wiped his eyes in disbelief. Another soldier screamed, clutching at an arrow in his chest, then fell backward with a splash.

"Indians!" someone yelled and everyone scrambled in panic for the riverbank. The naked soldiers grabbed their guns and looked around frantically but found nothing to shoot.

Baines and the other sergeant were more fortunate. The first arrow unleashed by the advancing Indians missed its mark, thudding into the wagon siding. The two sergeants grabbed their shotguns and threw themselves beneath the wagon. As the three Navajos rushed forward, the sergeants began firing. Two Indians dropped to the sand, mortally wounded, while Swift Arrow took a blast in his side.

He clutched the wound and staggered back to the tethered horses before another shot could be fired. He remembered the coyote that had crossed their path earlier in the day. It was a sign to turn back, but Swift Arrow had ignored it; now, he saw the folly of doing so.

The three friends helped Swift Arrow onto his horse and they galloped off as another bullet zinged over their heads.

The unclothed soldiers were still standing with their weapons ready when Sergeant Baines came through the trees with his gun.

"Well, we scared them redskins off, no thanks to you bathin' beauties!" he snarled.

Then he saw the two floating bodies and dropped the gun. He waded into the stream, took the dead men in each hand, and dragged them out, flopping the bodies onto the sand. The sergeant looked with disgust at the naked blanch-faced men.

"Two men dead!" Baines growled with contempt. "The next time one of you buzzards falls asleep on guard duty, he gets dragged by his feet the rest of the way to Fort Stanton! Now, git your clothes on and start diggin' graves for these men!"

It was a sobering experience for the men as they spent the rest of the day digging two graves. The dead soldiers were laid to rest while the sun eased below the horizon in a fading blaze of red and gold.

"What about those two dead Indians," Ben asked Sergeant Baines. "Shouldn't we bury them, too?"

"Naw," Baines replied. "Their buddies'll come back for 'em after we're gone."

Guards were posted for the night and, but even though their bodies were drained of energy, this time there was no sleeping on duty.

When Terry and Ben got their blankets ready, Ben rubbed his aching feet. "I kind of wish they would drag me by my feet the rest of the way!"

The black velvet sky was filled with stars so bright they seemed within reach. Terry breathed in the clean air that was scented with a touch of sage brush and wondered about the Indians who had ridden off after the day's attack. They knew the wagon and soldiers were still on the way—what if the Indians came back with reinforcements? Too exhausted to dwell on it, he soon fell asleep, numbed by the exciting and tragic events that had taken place on this second incredible day in New Mexico.

CHAPTER FOUR

Changing Woman's foreboding words still lingered in Willow-In-Storm's mind as she corralled the sheep and then went to the hogan to prepare her father's evening meal.

Later, while the last rays of sunlight were fading behind sacred *Tsoodzil*, the braves came in from their raiding. Willow-In-Storm heard the hoofbeats and went out with others to greet the young warriors. She gasped to see Swift Arrow draped over his horse. The three braves took him down and carried the wounded boy to his father's house. There was no time for the medicine man to prepare a design of colored sand on which to lay the injured brave, so the Trembling Hand ceremony was administered over Swift Arrow's unconscious body.

The old medicine man, or Singer as we he was called, began his magical chanting and ran shaking hands over the suffering young man in order to draw out the evil thing that had done him harm.

Willow-In-Storm lay in her hogan with wide-open eyes, listening to the Singer's repetitious words echoing through the village until finally the droning voice lulled her to sleep.

She was awakened in the early morning hours by the sound of her father breaking twigs to start a fire beneath the smoke hole. The village was quiet and she sat up with apprehension.

"I do not hear the Singer any longer!"

"The Singer is no longer needed," her father said. "Swift Arrow is better."

With relief, Willow-In-Storm went to Swift Arrow's hogan and his father came out with a tired but pleased expression.

"My son is awake now," the old man said. "You may see him, if you wish."

Willow-In-Storm went inside and knelt beside the wounded boy. "Is it true you have been healed?" she asked.

Swift Arrow gave her a painful look. "The Singer has chased away the demons. I will soon be riding my horse again."

She sat back on her heels with a tired sigh. "Yes, only to go on another raid. You see how it is? You could have been my husband, now. . .and I carrying your child. What if you were killed?"

"But I was not. I have protection from the Enemy Way."

"So did the other two who were with you, and they are dead, now."

He shook his head. "Perhaps it was ordained. . .only the Holy Ones know."

"And your time may be next!"

"I am not afraid. I must go out again and take more horses to buy you in marriage."

She got to her feet in anger. "I will not consider marriage until you show the white men you will live in peace!"

Swift Arrow was in no condition to argue and she left him to rest.

That night, Willow-In-Storm lay on her blanket but sleep would not come. She wished she had been born in the early days, after the sacred Dinetah had been given to her people. There were no white men at that time. The Diné were free to hunt, raise their cattle and grow their food. She was relieved that Changing Woman's prediction had been fulfilled after Chindi had visited the village with death. Perhaps, now, they would be able to live in peace.

Willow-In-Storm's dark eyes moved to the ceiling's smoke hole and she saw that the large full moon had placed itself in the very center. The strange markings on its ivory surface always carried the faint image of a human face, but now it seemed more so. As Willow-In-Storm gazed, its dark areas began to move slightly and were soon transformed into the face of a beautiful woman with shells at her ear lobes. Willow-In-Storm gasped, for she knew it was Changing Woman. The familiar voice entered Willow-In-Storm's heart once more and she lay, scarcely breathing.

"Things have not changed," the soft words told her. "This is only the beginning. A terrible journey lies ahead, but you must put love and courage in your heart before the sun can shine again for all the Diné."

CHAPTER FIVE

After a hundred and fifty miles of sun and dust, the weary soldiers straggled in like scarecrows behind the wagon and gaped at their new home.

Although Fort Stanton was still in ruins, most of the adobe walls still sat waiting for repairs. Only four buildings had been erected—a combination orderly room and post commander's quarters, an enlisted men's mess, an officers' mess and a sutler's store. All personnel, except the commander, slept in large tents. The entire settlement rested in the cool air and smell of pines, surrounded by mountains filled with juniper and piñon. Nearby gurgled the sparkling Bonito River while the Sierra Blanca rose in the west as a majestic background.

"You got your choice of beds," Sergeant Baines told the soldiers, "four men to a tent. The First New Mexico Volunteers have the ones over there. Roll call is at five o'clock and mess at six. Get plenty o' sleep, 'cause tomorrow you'll be helpin' the Volunteers put this place back together."

The large, roomy tents had a dirt floor, sprinkled and packed down shiny-hard with heated shovels, while the familiar iron-frame beds and their straw mattresses sat with a trunk at the foot of each. A sheet-metal stove, with its pipe sticking up through the center roof, offered heat during the cold nights.

When the men went to mess that evening, they sat with the New Mexico Volunteers at a long wooden table, the non-commissioned officers occupying one end. Terry and Ben expected the same dreary meal of beans, hardtack and coffee, but were surprised by fried venison and gravy, since fort personnel had killed two deer in the hills that day.

"This shore beats rattlesnake," Snake Eater Simmons said, and crammed his mouth full of deer meat.

One of the Volunteers laughed. "You're gonna find this place better than most other forts. Old Kit'll look after you here!"

Terry looked up. "Kit?"

"The commander—Colonel Kit Carson."

Terry remembered reading about the legendary mountain man. Of course, Kit Carson would be here—these men were the First New Mexico Volunteers, a group of local ranchers and farmers Carson had rounded up to help the Army fight the invading Confederates.

"Well, he sure has a nice place," Ben said.

The Volunteer chuckled. "You should've seen it when we first got here. The Union burned the fort last year t'keep Confederates from takin' it. We're still tryin' to put it back together!"

That night, Terry and Ben collapsed with aching bodies onto the hard straw mattresses for a long, needed sleep. However, it was cut short when Sergeant Baines walked up to Terry's cot. "You're needed in the orderly room, Private. Come on with me!"

Terry moaned. "But Sergeant, I've just walked half way across New Mexico!"

Sergeant Baines glared. "Do I hear guff comin' from that mouth o' yours?"

Terry sighed and put on his shoes. "I'm going, I'm going!"

The sergeant escorted Terry across the parade ground to the orderly room where he was shown a rough desk and chair.

"What am I supposed to do?" Terry asked.

"Take down anything that anybody has to report durin' the night. In the meantime, just sit down here and fill out the duty report."

Terry sat down and picked up a pencil. "What's a duty report?"

"The first sergeants bring in lists of their companies. You combine all the names on a sheet of paper." Baines took a paper from a stack on the desk. "Use this one as a guide."

Terry rubbed his eyes and yawned. "When is my duty over?"

"You'll be relieved in time for breakfast," Baines replied. "And don't fall asleep or you'll be court-martialed!"

After the sergeant departed, Terry squinted in the lamplight and began copying the soldiers' names on a piece of paper.

A moment later the door opened and a man dressed in casual Army uniform entered. His shirt was open at the collar and the rumpled coat unbuttoned. He was short for most men, only a little over five feet, barrel-chested and stood with the slightest hint of a stoop. His long reddish hair was streaked with silver while a heavy moustache of the same color drooped at the corners of his mouth.

Terry studied the man with half-closed eyes, then realized there was a colonel's insignia on the wrinkled uniform. Terry jumped to his feet.

The colonel's blue-gray eyes sparked. "Sit down, sit down!"

Terry took his seat again.

"Yer records say you used t'write fer a magazine back in New York," the colonel said.

"Yes, sir. . .Carper's Weekly," Terry replied.

"Well, the adjutant that does all my writin' took sick. Looks like he'll be out fer a spell. I need you to write a letter fer me."

"Yes, sir," Terry said and took a clean sheet of paper.

"Jest write down what I say, then rewrite it to sound good. I'll sign it later."

Terry held the pencil in readiness. "To whom is the letter addressed?"

"It's to General James H. Carleton, Commander of the New Mexico Department at Santa Fe."

Terry began writing.

"Jest t'let you know," the colonel went on, "I've got Fort Stanton in good enough shape t'start yer plan of action. The five companies o' my Volunteers are here, now, an' we're ready. I'm waitin' fer your further orders." He paused and waved a hand in the air. "Jest put whatever y'do at the end an' I'll be back t'sign it later."

Terry looked up. "And whose name will it be?"

"Colonel Christopher Carson, Commander of the First New Mexico Volunteers."

Terry gulped. "I can have it ready in a few minutes, Colonel Carson."

"Kit!" the colonel replied. "It's Kit to ever'body."

Terry watched speechless as Kit Carson left the room. It took only a short while to put the letter into military style and Terry waited eagerly until Carson returned a half hour later. Terry handed the letter to him.

"You'll have t'read it t'me," Carson said and gave the letter back to Terry.

Terry cleared his throat and read the letter:

"To The Honorable General James H. Carleton. I am pleased to report that the restoration of Fort Stanton has been accomplished to the stage where we are able to begin operations. The five companies of my New Mexico Volunteers have arrived and we await your further orders. Your obedient servant, Colonel Christopher Carson, Commander, First New Mexico Volunteers."

"Y'done good, boy," Carson smiled and signed the letter with a pen. "You're mighty good with words. I'd like to give orders fer you to take the adjutant's place till he's back on his feet, so you can do all my writin' fer me."

"I'd be proud to do so," Terry beamed.

"So you wrote fer Carper's Weekly? Don't tell me you're one o' those that wrote them stories about Kit Carson?"

"No, sir, but I've read some of the books about you."

"Oughten to believe all them things they write. I had a friend read some o' that stuff t'me once. . .all it did was make me laugh!"

Terry's fascination grew. "How many Indians have you really killed?"

Carson's eyes narrowed. "Y'mean how many did I have to kill? Seems like ever'body thinks all I did was t'come out here and start killin' ever' Indian I came across. Sure, there was some I killed, but I never took a life jest fer the fun of it. Anybody I killed was 'cause it had t'be done t'save my own skin."

"Then all those things they say about you aren't necessarily true?"

"I tell you what. . ." Carson cleared his throat as if to set the record straight. "I don't like a hostile redskin any better than you do. And when they're hostile, I've fought 'em hard as any man. But the white man's done hostile things t'them, as well. Why, these pore ignorant critters don't know no better than to follow suit. I've seen as much of 'em as any white man livin' and I cain't help but pity 'em."

He looked embarrassed from all the personal talk.

"Well, thanks fer writin' that letter," he said and walked to the door. "I'll let you know when I need you agin."

After Kit Carson left, Terry managed somehow to get through his duty in the orderly room without falling asleep. When the replacement arrived in the early morning, Terry walked to the mess room for breakfast before returning to his tent.

"You came just in time," the cook told him. "The others have already eaten—I was about ready to close down the stove."

Terry waited for his bacon, fried mush and bread, then took the plate and coffee to sit down at the long wooden table. At that moment a man in his early thirties, dressed in buckskin clothes, stuck his head inside the doorway. "Got any coffee left?" he asked the cook. "They're all out at the officers' mess."

"Yes, sir—still got a few hot cups."

The man entered and accepted a mug of hot coffee, then came over to the table and sat down across from Terry. "Mind if I join you? I'm Captain Nicholas Hodt."

Terry was chagrined. "Sorry, sir, I didn't recognize you as a captain. I'm Private Terry O'Neill."

Captain Hodt pulled a whiskey flask from his coat pocket and poured an ample amount into the coffee. "That's all right," he laughed. "The way we dress around here, nobody knows who's what. Kit Carson doesn't much care what we wear, as long as we do our job."

"I know what you mean. I hardly realized he was a colonel when we met last night."

As Nicholas Hodt leaned back in his chair and sipped the hot coffee, there was a slight blur in his gray eyes and Terry knew this wasn't the captain's first drink of the day.

"Well, old Kit never did put up with Army regulations," Hodt said. "That's why he gets along so well with the men."

Terry continued eating his breakfast. "I've read that he actually lived with the Indians once."

"That's right. For about eight years—never saw a white man all that time. In fact, he married a Blackfoot girl. Ol' Kit said she always had a bowl of hot water for his feet when he came in from hunting."

Terry was fascinated. "Are they still married?"

"No, she died giving birth to their only child—a little girl. She's dead, now, too. . .last year."

"Did Kit ever marry again?"

"Oh, yes. He had another Indian wife or two, and more children. Now, he's got a pretty Mexican wife and family living up in Taos." Hodt thought for a moment. "Let's see, now. . .I believe there's three boys and a girl. The oldest one ought to be about eleven, now."

"You must have known Kit Carson for some time," Terry said.

"I fought with him at Valverde. Now, that's when you'll see how tough he can be—during battle. He might seem quiet and easy going, but when the time comes to take command, he's like a regular juggernaut!"

"I guess I'll get a chance to find out when we start fighting the Indians."

Captain Hodt frowned. "That's something I didn't expect I'd be doing when I joined the Army."

"But somebody has to stop their raiding and killing," Terry countered. "Might as well be us."

"We wouldn't have to, if we'd all just act civilized."

"How do you mean?"

Captain Hodt gave him a serious look. "You ever hear about the massacre at Fort Fauntleroy?"

Terry shook his head and took another bite of food.

"I was there. I watched our *civilized* United States soldiers shoot down

innocent Navajos in cold blood. . .shove bayonets in the backs of squaws
. . .bash in the heads of babies."

Terry stopped eating and took a gulp of coffee.

Captain Hodt looked apologetic. "I'm sorry. Shouldn't talk that way
when a man's eating his breakfast." He finished his coffee and then took out
the flask again for a quick gulp. He got up to leave and grinned at Terry.
"Well, nice meeting you, Private O'Neill. I hope you won't have to kill any
Indians."

As Captain Hodt walked a bit unsteadily out of the mess room Terry
sat, thoughtfully finishing his coffee. In just the last few hours, two men had
drawn back a curtain to reveal the west as it really is; but it was only a hint
of what lay ahead. Terry realized he would be learning much more about
this strange and violent land.

CHAPTER SIX

"I don't want to make you worry," Ben Adams said as he and Terry ate breakfast, "but the men've been talkin'."

"About what?"

"About them having to do all the hard work while you're sitting in the Orderly Room writing for the colonel."

Terry looked up in surprise. "It wasn't my doing. Kit Carson just wanted me to handle his correspondence while the adjutant was sick."

"Oh, I know that, Terry," Ben said with embarrassment. "Heck, it don't make me no never mind, but those others. . .well, they're just jealous, I guess."

Terry shrugged. "Don't let it bother you, Ben. We're all doing the jobs we're best suited for, that's all there is to it."

"I just want you to watch out!"

When they finished breakfast, Ben went to the sutler's to purchase a bar of soap and Terry returned to the tent. Only Grizzly Taylor and Moony Calhoun were there, sprawled on their cots.

"Hello, Striker," Grizzly sneered as Terry entered. "Been nursin' the colonel agin?"

Terry stopped in puzzlement. "What do you mean by 'Striker'?"

"Ain't you been in the Army long enough t'know that a Striker kisses an officer's backside fer extra privileges?"

"I'm not kissing anybody's backside," Terry replied stiffly. "I'm just doing my duty. . .and I'm not getting any special privileges." He walked to his cot.

Grizzly got up and followed. "Don't tell me spendin' all that time with the commander ain't bein' a Striker!"

Terry turned to face him. "Colonel Carson wants me to take care of his correspondence. I didn't volunteer for the job. . .he asked me to do it. Now, if you can't handle that, it's not my problem!"

Grizzly bridled in anger. "Ain't nobody talks t'me like that, you little tadpole!" He gave Terry's shoulder a hard punch, sending him backward onto the cot.

Terry surged in anger and jumped to his feet, throwing a hard fist into Grizzly's large stomach. The man gave a surprised huff and swung a doubled-up hand to Terry's face. Terry reeled but did not fall. Moony rushed over to them.

"Give 'im a chance, Grizzly," Moony said. "You're bigger than he is!"

A ringing pain echoed through Terry's head and he went at Grizzly with both fists pounding at the big man's face. Grizzly grabbed him with two big arms and threw Terry back onto the cot.

Ben Adams had now entered the tent and saw his friend being attacked. He ran over to face Grizzly.

"Leave him alone, you bag of beef!" Ben shouted. "Pick on somebody your own size!"

Terry got to his feet and Grizzly started for him again, but Ben threw a foot under Grizzly's leg, sending the huge man sprawling to the floor. Terry picked up the trunk from the foot of his bed and broke it over Grizzly's head as personal articles scattered everywhere.

"What the hell's goin' on here?!" a voice roared from the doorway.

The men turned to see Sergeant Baines walking quickly toward them. Grizzly moaned and sat up, rubbing his head, while the others stood with innocent expressions.

"You all know fightin' ain't allowed in the tents!" Baines snarled. "Who's to blame for this?"

Moony tried to keep from smiling. "It was just an accident, Sergeant. Grizzly Taylor, here, seems to have stumbled over Private O'Neill's trunk, is all."

Sergeant Baines looked at each face and saw Terry's bruised eye. "Looks like O'Neill's the one done the stumblin'. Private, you better go to the dispensary and git somethin' put on that eye." He looked down at Grizzly Taylor. "And Taylor, you get another trunk from the Quartermaster for O'Neill and put his things back in—nice and neat—'cause I'm givin' all of you inspection in two hours!"

When Terry returned to his duties in the Orderly Room, Kit Carson's moustache raised in amusement at Terry's bruised and swollen eye. "Looks like you jest met up with a bear!"

Terry glanced down, embarrassed. "I guess you could say so—a grizzly!"

Carson was holding a paper and he gave it to Terry. "This jest came in from General Carleton. It's my first orders from the general an' I didn't want jest anybody t'see it. If you'd read it t'me, I'd be obliged."

Terry opened the envelope and read the contents aloud:

"It is imperative to put an end to the Indians' senseless raiding and killing of white men, women and children. Therefore, as Commander of the Department of New Mexico, I am ordering Colonel Christopher Carson, commander of the First New Mexico Volunteers, to start with the Mescalero Apaches. You will carry out the following:

"All Indian men of that tribe are to be killed whenever and wherever you find them. The women and children will not be harmed, but you will take them prisoners and feed them at Fort Stanton until you receive other instructions about them.

"You are being sent to punish the Indians for their treachery and their crimes; you have no power to make peace; you are there to kill them wherever you can find them. If they beg for peace, their chiefs and twenty of their principal men must come to Santa Fe to have a talk here. I will expect to receive word soon of your accomplishments in this regard."

When Terry finished reading he looked up, but Carson had turned his back, pulling at his moustache with agitation.

"This both shakes me down to my boots and embarrasses me!" Carson finally said quietly and turned around with worried eyes. "Fer one thing, I started the First New Mexico Volunteers to fight the Confederates, not the Indians. And I am embarrassed to turn against them that's put their trust in me."

Terry was surprised at the colonel's reaction. "But these are orders from your superior. . .what are you going to do?"

Carson thought for a moment. "I didn't go into this thing with the idea of killin' ever' male Indian I could find. But I have great respect fer General Carleton. . .he's doin' what he thinks best. If I don't follow orders, I'll be a traitor to my country. We'll jest have t'go after them Indians. Maybe when they see we mean business, they'll surrender with as little bloodshed as possible."

Kit Carson ordered two companies assembled immediately.

"General Carleton has given orders t'kill all the Apache men and take women and children prisoner," he told the commanders. "Now, I don't like the idea of shootin' the Indians outright. The general did say he was willin' to talk peace with any chief wantin' to do so, so I'm askin' you not t'do any killin' unless they refuse to surrender."

Ben Adams was one of the soldiers assigned to Company B, which was to leave the next morning, and he gave his gun a thorough check.

"Do you think you'll have to kill any Indians?" Terry asked him.

"I never shot a man," Ben said, "but if it's just an Indian, I guess it's not such a big thing."

The two companies rode out in the early morning. Ben Adams' unit didn't see any Indians until late afternoon when the company found about twenty men, women and children Apaches gathered at a campfire.

"Remember," the commander told his men, "if they won't surrender, we're to shoot only the men."

The soldiers bravely rode into the camp, knowing they were too many for the Indians to resist.

"The big white chief in Santa Fe wants you to do no more fighting and live in peace," the commander told the old Indian chief. "You're to surrender and come with us. If you refuse, we have orders to kill you!"

The old chief gazed at the commander with puzzled eyes, then turned to a younger Indian who obviously understood the white man's words. The two Apaches spoke to each other briefly and the younger one addressed the commander in English.

"Our chief says this is our land. We are living in peace now. There is no need to go with you."

The soldiers raised their weapons and Ben Adams' heart pounded while he fingered the trigger of his gun. Even though they were just Indians, it didn't seem right to kill them. A sweat broke out on his forehead.

"I will ask you one more time to surrender," the commander said. "Otherwise, my orders are to kill the men and take the women and children prisoners."

The young Apache translated the words to his chief and the Indian women clutched their children in fear as they listened.

The Indian looked back at the commander with defiant ebony eyes. "This is our land and our people will stay where we belong!"

"All right," the commander said and fired his revolver point blank at the chief.

The old man dropped to the ground with a deadly moan while the other soldiers, except Ben, started shooting. More Apaches fell, clutching at their chests. The Indian women screamed and grabbed their children. As they ran into the brush, the commander gave orders for them to be captured and the soldiers galloped after them.

When the two companies returned to Fort Stanton in late afternoon, Kit Carson went out to meet them. Terry followed and watched from a short distance.

Ten Indian women were being led by ropes behind the soldiers' horses. Some of the women's hands were bound while others held tiny children in their arms. The women's eyes were filled with terror and a few cried in agony over the loss of their husbands.

"They refused to surrender," one of the commanders told Kit Carson, "so we had to shoot 'em."

Carson ground his teeth. "Take the prisoners to the stables. Give 'em food and treat 'em well till I hear from General Carleton."

When Terry saw Ben Adams alone in the tent, he was anxious to hear about the Indian fight.

"I couldn't do it, Terry!" Ben said helplessly. "I just couldn't!"

Terry was surprised. "But you said you didn't mind killing an Indian."

Ben shook his head. "I know, but they were way outnumbered—it just didn't seem right to shoot 'em down!"

Terry breathed a sigh. "Ben, you can't let the others see you not stand up and fight. This is something that has to be done. Just keep in mind the next time, that they're savages who raid and kill white people—if you don't kill them, they'll kill you!"

Ben clenched his jaw. "All right, Terry, just don't badger me. I'll shoot one yet, but I cain't say I'll feel good doin' it!"

The following day, Snake Eater Simmons and Grizzly Taylor rode out with Company H, in the command of Captain James "Paddy" Graydon and his company of Volunteers.

Graydon was one of Kit Carson's close friends, and the two had bravely fought Confederates at the Battle of Valverde. Like Carson, Graydon was easy going and much admired by the men serving under him. With the same disregard for Army regulations as Kit Carson, Captain Graydon was most often called "Paddy," even by the lowest privates in his unit. Perhaps the most unredeemable part of Paddy Graydon's character was his strong dislike of the Indians.

Graydon led his Company H to the crest of a hill in the morning sun and called the men to a halt. A short distance below they saw a party of about twenty Mescalero men and one woman, riding their horses north.

"Draw your guns and proceed with caution!" Graydon ordered.

His company far outnumbered the Indians and the red men pulled their horses to a stop as the soldiers rode up with guns ready.

One of the old Indians raised his arm. "I know you are killing our people," he said. "I am Chief Manuelito and this is Chief Jose Largo. I ask that you do not kill us, for we go in peace to talk with your Big Chief in Santa Fe."

"The white man doesn't want to talk peace," Graydon told him gruffly.

"We got orders to kill all the men instead!"

He turned his pistol on Chief Manuelito and fired. The Indian grabbed his chest and slid from the horse with a groan. It was an unspoken command to start shooting and Grizzly fired his pistol at the other chief who fell mortally wounded. The remaining Indians wheeled their horses in panic but the other soldiers opened fire and four warriors, along with the woman, were gunned down. The other terrified Indians continued to ride off in panic, but the troops gave chase, shooting down five more Apaches.

Paddy Graydon and his men returned to Fort Stanton to report their victory.

"We took seventeen horses and mules and killed a dozen Indians," Graydon proudly told Colonel Carson. "Two of those killed were chiefs."

"Chiefs?" Kit said in surprise. "Do you know which ones?"

"Yes. One said he was Manuelito and the other was Jose Largo. Said they were goin' to Santa Fe to talk peace."

Kit Carson was startled. "Manuelito and Jose Largo were the two most important Apache chiefs. And you killed them when they said they were goin' t'talk peace?! Their talks with General Carleton could've meant a stop to this whole durned business!"

Paddy Graydon was perplexed. "But, Kit, the orders were not to accept any request to talk peace. . .to kill all the men. I did exactly as ordered!"

Carson puffed in disgust and lowered his head. "Yes, Paddy, those were the orders. Now, if you'll excuse me. . .and tell that Private O'Neill I need to see him."

Terry reported to Kit Carson and found him pacing the floor with hands behind his back. His stoop was more pronounced and when he turned around, his steely eyes were flashing.

"I want a letter sent to General Carleton as fast as it can get there," he said curtly.

Terry went quickly to the desk and grabbed a pencil and paper.

"Yer orders were duly received and carried out," Carson began. "Two different companies killed several Mescalero men and took three women and two children prisoners. But I feel this campaign is startin' off on the wrong foot. Today Captain James Graydon killed two of the biggest chiefs, Manuelito and Jose Largo, and several of their braves, plus a squaw. This, after they told Graydon they were goin' to Santa Fe t'talk to you about makin' peace. I find this action completely unfair and want to state my feelin's against it. I wait fer yer thinkin' on this matter."

After Kit Carson had signed the letter and it was sent by special courier to Santa Fe, further scouting was put on hold until an answer was received from General Carleton.

When word came back promptly, Terry read it to Carson:

"If you are satisfied that Graydon's attack on Manuelito and his people was not fair and open, see that all the horses and mules are returned to the survivors of Manuelito's band. In the meantime, you are to continue with my original orders."

Kit Carson banged his fist on the back of a chair. "Small payment to the families of them pore Indians who got murdered when they was lookin' t'make peace!"

That night Terry sat on his cot in the tent, penning a letter to his fiance Susan Godfrey.

"I'm trying to make sense of this whole thing," he wrote. "Before arriving in New Mexico, I had little opinion of the Indians—they were just savages and it seemed that killing them was of no real consequence.

"Our commanding colonel here at Fort Stanton is the famous mountain man Kit Carson. Even though he's fought and killed many Indians, he still respects them as human beings. Now, his superior, General Carleton in Santa Fe, has given him orders to kill all Apache men on sight and take the women and children prisoners.

"Kit Carson, is deeply grieved by having to inflict a deadly campaign against the people who have put their trust in him and I sympathize with him for having been pushed into such a dilemma by his iron-fisted commander.

"But I'm in the Army and my job is to kill the enemy, whether it's an Indian or a Confederate. I don't have any love for the Indians, so when the time comes, I know I won't be as hesitant to shoot as Colonel Kit Carson might be."

CHAPTER SEVEN

"Mornin', Private," the sutler store owner greeted Terry as he entered. "I jest opened up. Reckon you need more writin' paper?"

"That's right," Terry said, "but this is for me, so don't put it on the colonel's tab."

The owner pulled down a pad of paper. "I reckon ol' Kit keeps you mighty busy with all that writin'."

"Well, he has a lot of correspondence."

"I seen him ridin' out early this mornin' with a company o' men. Reckon he's chasin' Indians?"

"He's trying to find the other Apache chiefs. Wants to talk them into making peace without any more bloodshed."

The door opened and Captain Hodt came in. The sutler grinned knowingly. "Mornin', Captain. Jest gimme yer canteen and I'll fill it fer you."

Hodt handed over his canteen and the sutler started filling it from a whiskey barrel.

"I heard that Doc Whitlock rode in this morning," Hodt said. "Has he been around yet?"

The sutler looked up in alarm. "Whitlock?! What's he doin' here?"

Hodt chuckled. "Might be looking for Paddy Graydon."

The sutler stiffened in dread. "If those two see each other, there's gonna be trouble!"

Terry was curious. "What kind of trouble?"

"Old Doc Whitlock had a letter published in one of those Santa Fe newspapers," Captain Hodt replied. "He stated that Paddy Graydon and his company of soldiers got a bunch of Indians drunk and then killed them in cold blood."

The sutler added to the information. "And Paddy swore if he ever saw Whitlock, he'd make him retract that story or Paddy'd kill 'im!"

The sutler gave Hodt his canteen of whiskey and then looked through the front window. "Lordy, here comes Doc Whitlock, now!"

Hodt and Terry turned to the window and saw that a man in gray pants and a long dark coat had just ridden up. He tied his horse to a railing in front of the store and came inside.

"Why, hello there, Doc," the sutler greeted him with a forced smile. "What brings you to Fort Stanton?"

"Howdy, Luke," Whitlock said. "Lookin' for Kit Carson. Wondered if he'd hire me on as post surgeon, now that he's got his Volunteers rounded up again."

Captain Hodt answered, hoping the doctor would get back on his horse and ride away.

"The colonel's out on a scout today, Doc. Won't be back till late this afternoon. But I can tell you, now, we've already got a post surgeon over at the hospital."

Whitlock looked disappointed. "Well, I'd like to see Kit again, anyway, for old time's sake. I was his surgeon at the Valverde battle and we've been close friends ever since. Maybe I'll just hang around till he gets back."

Suddenly the sutler's face turned white as the door opened and Captain Paddy Graydon walked into the store. When Graydon realized who was standing before him, he stopped in his tracks with angry narrowed eyes.

"Well, if it ain't the libelous, slanderin' Doc Whitlock!" Graydon snarled. "I've been hopin' to run into you and make you eat all them lies you printed about me!"

Doc Whitlock stood his ground.

"I'll never go back on the truth," he said evenly. "I refuse to retract a single word, and if given the time and opportunity, I can prove everything I said about your despicable actions!"

Paddy Graydon glanced at Whitlock's pistol strapped to his waist. "I ain't got a gun, but if that's the way you feel, Doc, let me go get one and I'll challenge you to a duel. . .right here and now!"

"Go get your gun," Whitlock replied. "I'll wait for you in front of the officers' quarters."

Paddy Graydon turned and walked out of the store, then Whitlock followed. Terry joined Nicholas Hodt and the sutler as they went to the window to watch the showdown.

Doc Whitlock stood outside the officers' tents with his pistol drawn until Paddy Graydon came out with his own gun. Several of Graydon's men followed and stood at a respectful distance.

Whitlock didn't give Paddy Graydon a chance and quickly fired, but the bullet missed, zinging into a corner of a tent as the soldiers jumped aside. Graydon answered with a roar from his gun, shattering the stock of Whitlock's pistol and wounding him in the wrist. The doctor managed to let go another shot and Paddy Graydon grabbed at his chest in pain, then staggered backward as two of his men ran to catch him. They carried their wounded captain back into the tent.

Doc Whitlock threw down his broken gun and rushed back into the sutler's store. Terry, Nicholas Hodt and the sutler watched as the doctor grabbed a shotgun from a nearby gun rack. He took some shells from the rack and loaded the gun. No one said a word as Whitlock stood looking through the doorway.

It was only a moment before a group of Paddy Graydon's men came marching toward the store, waving pistols in the air.

"You killed Paddy!" one of them cried. "Now, it's your turn, Whitlock!"

The doctor saw he was outnumbered and turned to rush out the back door as the men entered. Shots rang out and Doc Whitlock fell through the open door, his body full of bullet holes.

Terry stood wide-eyed as the men dragged Doc Whitlock to the back door and threw him into a ditch. Then, one by one, Paddy Graydon's men walked by with heated revenge and fired a bullet into Whitlock's body.

Terry had seen enough. He clutched his pad of writing paper and hurried out of the store as more of Paddy Graydon's unit arrived, carrying pistols, rifles and shotguns. Terry could hear more gunshots, one after another, as he ran all the way back to his own tent.

It was late afternoon when Kit Carson and his unit returned from an unsuccessful scouting mission and only Captain Hubbell of G Company came out to greet the colonel.

"The place is mighty quiet," Kit Carson said. "Where is ever'body?"

"We've had a bit of trouble here today," Captain Hubbell said.

Carson looked around at the almost deserted post. "What kind of trouble?"

Captain Hubbell took a deep breath and continued. "Old Doc Whitlock stopped by to see you. Unfortunately, he and Paddy Graydon saw each other and words were exchanged."

Carson's eyes narrowed. "I know there's bad feelin' between them two," he said. "It must've been more'n words that were exchanged!"

Hubbell lowered his eyes. "That's right, colonel. I'm afraid they're both dead."

"What?!" Carson sputtered and got down quickly from his horse. "Jest what happened?"

"Well, you see they challenged each other to a duel. Whitlock shot and killed Paddy. . .then Paddy's men killed the Doc."

Carson's anger simmered. "Where are they?" he demanded.

"The post surgeon has them over at the hospital."

The captain followed Carson as he went quickly to the hospital to verify the incredible news that two of his good friends had been murdered.

"Their bodies are in the other room," the post surgeon told Carson, "but you wouldn't want to see Doc Whitlock's. I've never seen anything like it. . .he's been riddled by at least a hundred and fifty gunshots!"

Kit Carson erupted in rage. "Git Companies G and H on the parade ground this instant!" he shouted at Captain Hubbell.

In the dark shadows of late afternoon, the two companies of soldiers gathered hurriedly to attention in front of the officers' quarters. Terry O'Neill watched from his tent as Kit Carson stomped back and forth with hands clasped behind his back.

"Captain Hubbell," Carson roared, "have yer men of Company G remove every firearm from each one o' the so-called 'men' in Company H. I mean every one, down to the last private in the rear ranks!"

Carson stood with an angry pounding heart as the guns were taken away from the Company H soldiers. When it was done, he glared in fury at the unarmed men and bellowed, "I'll have you scoundrels swing before sunset!" He turned and stomped to his quarters.

Neither Terry nor any other soldier, even those who had served with Kit Carson the longest, had ever seen the man in such a towering, threatening rage. Captain Hubbell and other long-time associate officers of Carson gave the colonel a few minutes to cool down, then they went to advise him.

"Kit, you mustn't let your anger make you resort to unmilitary action," Captain Hubbell said. "If you return violence with violence, even though it seems justified, it could mean the end of your career."

Another old friend spoke up. "We agree that some sort of punishment should be given, but you can't hang the entire Company H. Wouldn't it be better to have only the ring leaders who instigated this terrible act arrested? Have them taken to Albuquerque and held in jail for trial."

The fire of Carson's wrath began to fade and he shook his head in despair over the deaths of two close friends.

"You're right," he sighed. "You're right, all of you. But I don't wanna see another hair o' them scoundrels' heads! Have those men put in irons and git 'em out of my fort as soon as you can!"

CHAPTER EIGHT

Ben Adams was not thrilled with the prospect of another Indian fight.

"I heard we got orders from that general in Santa Fe to go in a radius of a hundred miles, looking for Apaches!" he said to Terry. "My company's going southwest, looking fer Gilas. How about you, I guess you'll be going with Kit Carson's party?"

Unlike Ben, Terry was excited about going on his first hunt. "No, the colonel's riding follow-up. I'm going with Captain William McCleave and two companies to the southeast. We're supposed to find the Mescaleros."

Ben swallowed hard. "Well, anyway, I'll be looking for you to come back all right, now, you hear?"

Captain McCleave's two companies rode first through the Sacramento Mountains, with no trace of Mescaleros, then moved south to the Guadalupe Mountains. They found their prey at a place called Dog Canyon.

"There's probably five hundred Indians camped in that hollow a mile ahead," the advance scout reported in a hushed voice. "I didn't see any guards, so maybe they haven't seen us yet."

"All right," Captain McCleave replied quietly, "we'll try to block them in." He didn't want to shout to his men, so he turned to a sergeant. "Have one company ride unnoticed to the other end of the canyon and move in. The rest of us will enter from this end. . .they won't be able to get away. Remember, shoot all the men and take the women and children captive!"

After half the soldiers had ridden around to the opposite mouth of the canyon, Terry felt a ripple of excitement as he and the others charged their horses forward with maniacal shouts.

It was a pitiful one-sided battle. The Indians were completely surprised and didn't have a chance with only their bows and arrows against the soldiers' rifles. Among the screams and yells of fighting, the Indians were shot down in cold blood as they tried to escape. Terry spotted an Apache man trying to help some women and children climb the canyon's steep walls, but the warrior was felled with a bullet and, as he lay wounded, Army horses trampled him to death under their sharp hooves.

The unfairness of it all swept over Terry and he held back from shooting while the horrible din of battle swirled around him. Then he saw a fallen Apache with a bow and arrow aimed straight at his heart. Terry didn't even have to take aim. It was like shooting rabbits with his father; he simply raised the rifle and fired. The Indian fell back, twitching on the ground in the throes of death.

Some of the Indians were able to ride through the flank of soldiers and escape, but the Apaches had suffered a great loss. Captain McCleave's men took captive the few women and children left behind and returned to Fort Stanton.

Ben Adams' unit had already come back and Ben was lying wearily on his cot when Terry straggled into the tent.

"How did it go?" Terry asked, dumping his pack and rifle. "Did you do any fighting?"

"Yes," Ben replied glumly. "We ran across a couple of camps, killed a bunch and took some women captives." He looked at Terry. "Did you kill any?"

"Yes, I shot a few."

Ben stared at the ceiling and there was a moment while neither spoke. Finally, Ben asked, "How did it feel, Terry. . .when you killed one of them?"

Terry shrugged. "With everybody shooting, I didn't have time to think about it. I just kept shooting like the others." He saw the agony in Ben's eyes. "I know how you feel about killing, Ben, but heck, they're only Indians!"

"But they're people, Terry," Ben said quietly, "the same as you and me. I keep wondering if the man I killed had a family. . .maybe a wife and children who are all alone, now."

"But he would've killed you—you had to get him first!"

Ben's lack of response made Terry uncomfortable. "Ben, we're in the Army and that's what we're supposed to do. You're just going to have to live with it!"

Terry heaved a sigh of agitation and walked out of the tent. A small feeling of guilt stuck in his throat and he looked for something to kick.

CHAPTER NINE

Willow-In-Storm placed two bowls of mutton stew before her father and his brother Standing Bear. She was always proud to serve her uncle, not only because he was headman of the clan, but she felt it her duty to cook for him occasionally since his wife had been taken away some time ago. Now, she was bothered to see the worry on her uncle's face.

"I have been told that the Mescalero Apaches in the south are being murdered by the white man's army," Standing Bear said as he began to eat. "Many of us are concerned."

"But the Apaches are our enemies, like the Utes from the north," his brother replied. "They take our horses and sheep in the night. We should not care what happens to them."

"The white man's fort has been restored and is now filled with many new soldiers," Standing Bear continued. "Many of our people fear that after the white men kill the Apaches, they will swarm to the north like so many bees and do the same to the Diné."

Willow-in-Storm listened in dread and recalled Changing Woman's ominous words. "Then we will suffer another war and lose many of our people!"

"Many of our young braves are eager to raid and kill, which makes the white men even more anxious to do us harm," Standing Bear said. "The braves will not listen to me, so I have asked the headmen of all clans to hold council here tomorrow. Even Manuelito will be here. . .perhaps they will listen to him."

The Navajo Manuelito, bearing the same name as the Apache Chief Manuelito killed near Fort Stanton by the white soldiers, was highly respected by all the Indians of northern New Mexico.

"I hope you are right," Willow-In-Storm's father said. "Manuelito is the greatest headman of all the clans. But the young men know that he is a *rico*. Being a rich one, with many fine cattle, he has no need to raid or kill."

When the headmen from surrounding clans arrived the next day, they gathered in a large hogan and sat in a circle around the fire pit to discuss the dark cloud on their horizon.

"We cannot be sure what is in the mind of the white men," Standing Bear told the group, "but if we wait to find out, it may be too late. I suggest that we move farther to the northwest, just in case."

Manuelito listened as he sat proudly erect with strands of turquoise resting on his bare chest.

"I have never done the white man any wrong," he said. "I have never raided a settlement, for I am able to live off my own resources. The rest of you may run and hide, but I will never abandon our Dinetah."

"We would still be within Dinetah's boundary of the four sacred mountains," Standing Bear said. "My plan is to move to the area of *Tseghahodzani*, which the white men call Window Rock. That is where our medicine men get water for their rain ceremonies—the Holy Ones would surely protect us there."

Two of the headmen sided with Manuelito and refused to be chased away from their rich grazing land, preferring to continue the raids on white settlements.

One old but wise headman, however, spoke up. "I agree with Standing Bear. If the white men bring their killing this way, we will have been gone by that time. And at *Tseghahodzani* we will be hard to find. The white men will think we have disappeared."

A murmur ran through the circle and they all nodded, except for Manuelito and the other two obstinate headmen.

A gloom had settled over the village when Willow-In-Storm began helping her father and Standing Bear gather together the few belongings they would take with them on the trip northwest. The horses were soon loaded and the people ready to start the slow journey. Willow-In-Storm had just strapped a bundle onto her back when Swift Arrow came to say goodbye.

"As soon as I get enough horses, I will come for you," he told her.

She shook her head. "No, it will not work. You will always be raiding and killing. That is not the wish of my father's brother, and I agree with him. I will not marry you, only to see you killed and my children taken for slaves."

Swift Arrow squared his shoulders in proud anger. "Then so be it! Go with the others and hide like frightened squirrels. I will stay and fight with the braves who follow me!"

Willow-In-Storm glared back. "I do what my heart tells me. If it is wrong, then I will suffer the blame!" She adjusted the bundle on her back. "It is clear we must go separate ways. This is the last time our eyes will ever meet!"

She left him to join the others and Swift Arrow watched his people trudging out of the area on their way to an uncertain fate in northwestern Dinetah.

CHAPTER TEN

The morning was hot and dusty as six Mescalero Apaches approached Fort Stanton, one holding a stick with a white cloth attached. The sentinels held their fire and watched curiously as the Indians stopped a few feet away.

"We must speak with 'Keet' Carson," the one holding the truce flag announced loudly. "We want to make peace!"

The two guards looked at each other.

"Somebody go get the colonel," one of them said. "And for God's sake, don't shoot—we don't want the Old Man on our tails for killin' another Indian lookin' to talk peace!"

Word spread throughout the fort that there were Indians outside and a number of soldiers quickly massed at the entrance with guns ready. Terry, Ben and the others watched as the red men stood patiently in the warming sun. Kit Carson appeared and walked out to meet the Indians.

"Greetings, Gian-Nah-Tah," Carson said to the old Indian. "Good to see you again. They tell me you want t'talk peace."

The leather-faced Indian looked Kit Carson deep in the eyes. "You were once a friend. Now, you murder many Apaches in the hills and canyons. You guard the water holes so we have no food or water. That means you want to kill all our people. If that is your wish, then we surrender. Make peace. Stop killing."

"I don't have the authority t'talk peace," Carson told him. "If you want to do that, my orders are fer you and your men t'go to Santa Fe and talk with the Big White Chief, General Carleton."

The old Indian's stolid expression did not change, but his eyes clouded. "Chief Manuelito and Chief Jose Largo tried that and you killed them!"

"That was a mistake, and I'm sorry fer that. But I'll have soldiers escort you to Santa Fe so you'll be safe."

The Indian studied Carson before replying. There was a time when the Indians could believe this white eyes, but now, there was doubt. "I come back tomorrow with three important chiefs. Then we go to talk."

"I want to send an Indian agent with you to Santa Fe," Carson said. "It'll take a few days to round him up, along with the escorts. If you'll come back in three days, we'll be ready."

As soon as the Indians left, Kit Carson called for Terry O'Neill and dictated a letter to General Carleton, informing him of the subsequent visit by the Indians. Then Carson thankfully put a hold on all scouting parties until results of the Santa Fe meeting were known.

When Kit Carson signed the revised letter, he said to Terry, "I reckon General Carleton'll send his written report of the meeting back with the party, but I'd like a first-hand account. You're real good at puttin' words together, O'Neill, so I want you t'go as one of the escorts an' give me a detailed report when you get back."

Terry was pleased with the assignment. "I'd be very happy to do that," he said.

After the Indian Agent Lorenzo Labadie had arrived, the old Indian Gian-Nah-Tah returned to Fort Stanton as promised. Along with him were three important chiefs, Cadette, Chatto and Estrella. Captain Nicholas Hodt was placed in command. With Sergeant Baines, Terry and another soldier, the party started riding north on a cold November morning.

The Agent Labadie and Captain Hodt were in the lead while Terry, Sergeant Baines and the other soldier took up the rear. The four Indians rode in between and did not speak, even when camp was made the first night.

The group wrapped themselves in blankets to shut out the cold and ate their meal of meat, bread and coffee around a flickering campfire. The only sound was a crackle of burning twigs and the occasional howl of a coyote wandering the dark hills to the west. When time came to bed down, Sergeant Baines assigned a soldier for guard duty and Gian-Nah-Tah finally spoke in his own tongue to the Agent Labadie who answered, also in Apache.

Sergeant Baines was curious. "What did he say?"

"He says there's no need for guards, that his people know all the big chiefs are with us. Besides, if they attacked, they know Kit Carson would take great revenge."

Baines spat into the fire. "I don't care what he says, I'm postin' a guard every three hours."

When the group finally arrived at the capital of Santa Fe, the streets were coming alive as they entered the city. Quaint adobe buildings radiated from a central plaza where burro trains were bringing in Taos whiskey, foodstuffs and stove wood in a never ending procession. Three sides of the plaza were occupied by merchants and traders and the little stalls began filling up with onions, red and green peppers, apples, peaches and bundles of corn husks used for cigarette wrappers. The aroma of tobacco, fresh bread and sides of beef wafted across the plaza where the government administration building, called The Palace, took up the entire north side.

Even before the Indians came to see him, General Carleton had decided what he was going to do with them. By his direction, Fort Sumner was in construction beside the northern Pecos River where all the Indians would be placed on a reservation by a circular grove of cottonwood trees, called Bosque Redondo.

The motley group looked out of place as they stood in General Carleton's office where the old Indian Gian-Nah-Tah, in his better command of English, spoke for the others.

"It is clear that the white eyes are stronger than us and you have better weapons," Gian-Nah-Tah told Carleton. "If you give us like weapons and turn us loose, we will fight you again. Our spirit is not lacking, but we are hunted down and starved. We have no more heart. Do with us as may seem good to you, but do not forget. . .we are men and braves!"

Terry O'Neill stood aside with the others, listening. He realized how difficult it must be for these Indian chiefs to face General Carleton with dignity, to admit defeat and place the lives of their people in the white man's hands.

General Carleton met the eloquent speech with a grim smile. "It is good that you agree to let us help you," he said. "I have prepared a new home for you. . .east, on the Pecos River. It is called Bosque Redondo. I want you to return to your people and tell them that peace will come only if they submit to going to this place. There, your people will be fed and protected by the soldiers of Fort Sumner." Then Carleton clenched his fist. "But if any of you choose to remain in your homeland, Colonel Kit Carson's troops will hunt you down like animals and kill all of you!"

The general's fierce countenance and threatening speech created a negative impression in Terry's mind. It seemed the man could have stated his terms in a more gentle manner, but maybe it was necessary to do it this way. Even so, Terry felt a certain respect for the humbled Indians as the party started back to Fort Stanton.

During camp the first night, Terry sat with Captain Hodt and Agent Labadie by the fire as they consumed their usual unappetizing meal. Terry looked with concern at Gian-Nah-Tah who was eating with the other Indians some distance away.

"Mr. Labadie," Terry said to the Indian Agent next to him, "do you think there'll really be peace in the Territory, now?"

Lorenzo Labadie sipped his hot coffee. "If peace ever comes to this country, I don't think I'll be around to see it."

"But if all the Indians go to a reservation, it should stop the raids and killing."

Nicholas Hodt shook his head as he took out the whiskey flask. "Those Indians, there, represent only a fraction of the Apache tribes," he said. "There's the Mescalero, the Jicarilla, the Gila and many more—not only in New Mexico, but in Arizona, too. Then, there's the Navajo and Utes up north." He lifted the flask for a good swig.

"I see what you mean," Terry answered sadly. "It will take a long time."

"In my opinion, it depends on the white men more than the Indians," Hodt added. "If all of us could meet them on the same level, there'd be no problem."

Agent Labadie gave a helpless chuckle. "That's a nice dream, but it just doesn't seem to work. On several occasions I've brought everybody together and both sides promised to stop all this back-and-forth fighting. Then some darn-fool group of Anglos or Mexicans comes along to raid the Indian villages, steal their cattle and kidnap their women and children to sell as slaves. What else can the Indians do but retaliate? The whole thing just starts up again."

"It all sounds kind of hopeless," Terry said.

Labadie gave a tired sigh. "Maybe General Carleton's right. This Bosque Redondo thing might be a start. . .I'll give it a try, anyway."

CHAPTER ELEVEN

Terry watched with concern as over four hundred Mescalero Apaches began straggling into Fort Stanton for transportation to the Bosque Redondo reservation.

Most of them were hungry and only a few had blankets to protect them from the early winter cold. The Indians quickly set up temporary shelter, then sat forlornly in little bunches trying to warm themselves around their tiny fires.

Extra rations had been shipped in, anticipating the Indians' arrival, but it was scant and what little they received was strange to them.

"They don't know what to do with coffee beans," Terry advised Colonel Carson. "I saw one old woman boiling the beans and throwing out the dark water. When she couldn't chew the beans, she threw them out, too. I had to show them how to grind the beans first."

Carson nodded in worry. "Yes, and I hear they've been mixin' the flour with water, then eatin' it and gettin' sick. I've sent some men out t'kill a few deer—maybe that'll help 'em."

Kit Carson and the Indian Agent Lorenzo Labadie were disappointed that there weren't enough deer in the hills to feed everyone. When Carson heard reports of a few Indians dying, he dictated a message to General Carleton.

"The Indians are out of their environment," Terry wrote for him, "and dyin' from lack of proper food. We have to get 'em to Bosque Redondo as soon as possible where they can be properly fed. I'm still waitin' fer more wagons to start 'em on their way."

General Carleton's reply was prompt and heartless:

"No more wagons are available. Start the Indians on their way to Bosque Redondo immediately, on foot if necessary. If they can move, make them walk."

After reading the letter, Terry recalled his own grueling walk from Santa Fe.

"Why it's a good hundred miles," he told the colonel, "and the few wagons going on the trip will be loaded with supplies."

Carson's face was dark and expressionless. "We'll jest have t'make room fer the old and the sick. The important thing is t'git 'em to the Bosque before any more die on us!"

Icy November winds were sweeping down from the snow-covered mountains when the first group of Apaches assembled to leave for Bosque Redondo. Fifty soldiers were to ride as escorts, two of them being Deacon Jones and Moony Calhoun from Terry's tent quarters. Terry and Ben wrapped themselves in their greatcoats and went out to watch as everyone shivered from the biting cold. Half-naked Indian children huddled against their mothers for warmth while those lucky enough to have blankets, pulled them high around their necks.

Terry saw that almost all the four hundred Mescaleros were on foot; there was room in the wagons for only a few who could barely stand, let alone walk. Old men and women used gnarled tree limbs as walking sticks while babies were either carried in their mothers' arms or strapped in cradle boards on their mothers' backs. The Indian Agent Labadie, who was going with them, mingled with the group, trying to give them hope for a better situation at Bosque Redondo.

Deacon Jones and Moony Calhoun rode by, looking like two large bears huddled in their coats, and Ben Adams shouted to them.

"Hey Deacon, don't you and Moony freeze your backsides off before you get there!"

Moony blew on his cold hands and yelled back. "You better git back to your tents and start warmin' yours, 'cause you'll be comin' along next!"

They rode off and Ben looked around at the wretched crowd. "They sure got a pitiful bunch to herd," he muttered in a cloud of frost.

Terry gritted his teeth. "This is crazy—you know they're not all going to make it!"

Even as the large group was leaving, more Mescaleros poured into the fort and set up their meager living quarters. Kit Carson watched with frustration and could see the whole ugly process starting over again. While the Indians grew sick from hunger and cold, he had Terry write another letter.

"To General James Carleton," Carson began. "Things ain't goin' well fer the Indians, like you an' me would want. We're gettin' too many of 'em here at the fort to feed 'em right and some are dyin'. Not only that, a lot of the old and sick cain't walk and I still don't have enough wagons. As fer myself, I am totally discouraged. I haven't seen my wife and children fer close to a year. Duty, as well as happiness, directs me to my home and family and I trust that the General will accept my resignation."

Terry looked up in surprise.

"Well, that's probably not the right words t'use," Carson said with irritation, "but that's the way I feel! Jest put it the way it oughta be an' I'll sign the durned thing!"

Terry, Ben and the other soldiers kept doling out the meager rations and tried to show the Indians how to make the best of the strange food. Another letter came from General Carleton allowing Colonel Kit Carson two weeks leave to visit his family, but there was one stipulation—Carson must first stop in Santa Fe to talk with the general.

Kit Carson was anxious to see his family again and prepared to leave immediately.

"I don't know what General Carleton has to say," he told Terry before leaving, "but if he accepts my resignation, I reckon I won't be comin' back." He shook Terry's hand in farewell. "You're doin' good, boy. If I ever do get back, I'll see to it you git upped in rank!"

It was obvious that Kit Carson felt defeated by the whole Mescalero affair and Terry suddenly realized how much he admired the man.

Chapter Twelve

Deacon Jones and Moony Calhoun huddled in their greatcoats and rode glumly behind the double line of Mescalero Apaches struggling in misery across the frozen plains. After a few Indians at the end of the line had slipped away to return to their homeland, Deacon and Moony were now assigned to guard the rear.

Before leaving Fort Stanton, Moony had felt little concern for the Indians; they were just an ignorant people the Army had to deal with by herding them to a reservation. Now, after seeing the older ones drop to their knees with numbed and bloody feet, he thought otherwise.

"Hell," he said with disgust, "they oughta let some o' these old ones go. If they don't die here, they'd die anyway, tryin' to get back!"

Deacon stared soberly ahead and replied with determination, "We got our orders to git as many of 'em to the reservation alive as we can."

Moony watched an old Indian woman and her husband pushing themselves forward with walking sticks, trying to keep up with the others. Finally, the woman collapsed on the hard ground, her feet staining the sand with blood, and the man knelt to comfort his gasping wife. Deacon and Moony pulled their horses to a halt as the Indian Agent Lorenzo Labadie rushed out of line to check on the suffering Indians.

In a moment the captain in charge arrived on his horse. "What's holding you up?" he demanded.

"The woman's feet are bleeding and frozen," Labadie told him. "She can't walk any more."

The old Indian man, kneeling beside his wife, looked up with pleading eyes at the white men.

"We can't detain the party," the captain told the agent. "Now, Mr. Labadie, why don't you get back in line with the others. I'll take care of the situation."

Labadie hesitated, then got up in defeat to join the rest who were moving on. He shook his head as he walked past Deacon and Moony sitting on their horses.

"What y'reckon the captain's gonna do?" Moony asked in a low voice.

"I don't wanna find out," Deacon muttered. "Come on, let's git back with the rest of 'em."

They galloped off to take their places at the end of the line and continued at a slow trot. In a moment two gun shots cracked the air from behind and Moony stiffened; neither wanted to look back.

"He ain't jest shootin' coyotes," Deacon said.

The group was blessed with warmer weather when they reached the northern Pecos River, but the water was frigid.

"Soon's we git across this danged river," Deacon said, "we oughta be through travelin'. Fort Sumner's supposed t'be on the other side."

"About time!" Moony replied. "I been waitin' fer a warm barracks and a soft bed!"

A suitable spot was found to cross the river, but the Indians refused to walk into the freezing water. Agent Labadie tried coaxing, telling them that they would find food and shelter on the other side, but it was no use. Finally, the soldiers had to poke their gun barrels into the Indians' backs, forcing them into the icy stream. Moony wanted to at least carry some of the babies on his horse, but knew it was against regulations, so he watched the mothers hold their children high out of the water as they struggled to the other side.

When they finally reached Fort Sumner and the Bosque Redondo reservation, Deacon and Moony gazed at their new home in utter disappointment.

"This is a fort?!" Moony growled.

The establishment was nothing more than a few tents, housing three companies of men, while the newly arrived soldiers would have to sleep in their own dog tents.

The Indians found even more despair. After being herded in a line to be counted, they were given stale bread and water as a reward for trudging over a hundred miles across the freezing desert. To add to their misery, only a few threadbare blankets were issued and there was no housing of any kind waiting for them. While they shivered with hunger in a cold breeze, Agent Labadie went in anger to see Captain Joseph Updegraff, Fort Sumner's commanding officer.

"I am appalled!" Labadie told the commander. "The government promised to give these Indians a decent home with food, clothing and protection. I've brought them here in good faith and find nothing!"

Updegraff was likewise disgruntled.

"It's not my doing, I assure you," he replied. "When I surveyed this area with the others, we wanted to establish Fort Sumner at another place, with clear water, firewood and closer to Fort Union for supplies. But you evidently don't know General Carleton—he had decided on Bosque Redondo and no one can change Carleton's mind!"

"But what about food?" Labadie asked. "These Mescaleros have walked over a hundred miles on short rations and they're starving!"

Updegraff was stern but shrugged hopelessly. "Supplies haven't arrived like they should. I expect a shipment in the next day or two."

"And the homes the Indians expected to have waiting for them?"

"We haven't received that material either. In the meantime, General Carleton advises that the Indians should make do with what they can find to build shelters."

Agent Labadie went back to the miserable Apaches and helped them work in icy winds, putting up crude jacals that served mostly as windbreaks with little warmth.

Deacon Jones and Moony Calhoun put up their own little tents, along with the other newcomers, and looked forward to a hot meal. However, when they went to the mess tent they were served cold beans and mush with luke-warm coffee.

"We ain't eatin' any better than the Indians!" Moony complained.

One of the soldiers who had arrived earlier at Fort Sumner shook his head. "They keep tellin' us it'll get better. But supplies still ain't comin' in like they promised."

Deacon stirred the cold beans and shook his head. "This shore ain't what I had in mind when I volunteered to come west!"

CHAPTER THIRTEEN

Kit Carson's home in Taos, only seventy miles north of Santa Fe, made it convenient for him to stop for his visit with General Carleton. After the two shook hands in a warm greeting, Carson settled himself tiredly in a chair beside the general's desk.

"Cheer up, Colonel," Carleton said. "Things are going better than you think. As soon as we gather all the Mescalero Apaches at Bosque Redondo, you'll see they'll be happy and properly taken care of."

"Now that the Apaches have started fer the reservation," Carson replied, "I'd still like you to consider my resignation."

Carleton seemed not to have heard. "It was easy getting the Mescaleros to surrender," he continued, "but it couldn't have been done without your superior handling of the matter. Now, we have our greatest challenge ahead—forcing the Navajos to surrender and sending them to the Bosque with the Apaches."

Kit Carson looked up in surprise. This second plan, had never been mentioned, and he squinted his sharp eyes at the general.

"But the Navajos and Apaches are enemies. Gettin' 'em together is jest askin' fer trouble!"

"We'll keep them separated in their own camps. The soldiers will see to it that there's no trouble." Carleton leaned forward with eager eyes. "Besides, I plan to keep all of them busy plowing the land, planting seeds and growing their own crops. We'll teach the children to read and write and convert the Indians to Christianity. Don't you see what a perfect place Bosque Redondo will be?" He raised his eyes in self-adulation. "I could even call it 'Fair Carletonia!'"

Kit Carson knew the ways of the Indians and could see a multitude of problems ahead.

"You got a steep hill to climb, General," he said evenly. "Fer one thing, the Apache never was one to plow the land and grow his food. And they're nomads. . .you're gonna have one heck of a time holdin' 'em down in one place!"

"We can force them to learn the ways of the white man."

"And what about the Navajo *ricos?*" Carson argued.

"*Ricos?*"

"That's what they call the rich ones. The big chiefs with lots of cattle. They don't need to steal. They live peaceful. If they're not doin' any raidin' or killin', why make them go to the Bosque reservation?"

Carleton frowned with determination. "There will be no exception. *All* Navajos will go to the reservation!"

Carson shifted with agitation. "Some o' them headmen are mighty stubborn. The biggest one is Manuelito. . .same name as the Apache chief that was killed. Another big Navajo headman is Barboncito. This is their God-given land and if I know them two, they'll fight you to the last man!"

Carleton's face became threatening. "Then we'll fight them back. . .to the last man!"

Kit Carson saw that he was beating a stone wall and sat back in silence.

Now, General Carleton brought in his final weapon of flattery and patriotism that always worked with Kit Carson.

"I know it can be done," he said, "but only if you work with me. After all, Kit, you're the only man in New Mexico capable of directing this campaign. And remember, as a colonel and a soldier, you have an obligation to your superior and your country!" He fixed his riveting eyes on Carson. "I trust you'll see, then, why I cannot accept your resignation."

Before leaving Santa Fe for the short ride to his home in Taos, Kit Carson purchased a pretty shawl for his wife and peppermint sticks for the children. It was late afternoon when he rode up to the long adobe building that housed many families, one of which was the modest Carson residence.

His seven-year-old daughter Teresina saw him first; she was sitting by the front door, cradling a much-loved doll her father had made for her years before. Playing in the dirt beside her was four-year-old Kit Junior.

"Papa!" the girl cried in a burst of delight and jumped up to grab Carson's leg before he had a chance to get out of the saddle. "Did you bring me a present?"

Little Kit ran to clutch the other leg.

Carson looked down with a fond laugh. "Well, we'll never find out if the two of you don't let me get off my horse!"

The children stood back reluctantly and Teresina squealed, "Come down, come down, I want to see!"

The front door opened and a lovely Mexican woman in her mid-thirties stepped out to investigate the commotion. Her black eyes ignited at the sight of the man climbing down from his horse.

"*Por fin!*" she exclaimed. "*Querido Esposo!*"

Kit Carson made his way to her with difficulty while the children clung to his waist.

"Chipita!" he said, using the pet name for his wife, and gave her a kiss.

Teresina tugged impatiently at her father's coat. "Papa, I want to see my present!"

"All right, little badger," he told her, "let me tie up my horse, then we'll go inside and see what you can find."

He tethered his horse, took a package from the saddlebags and they all went into the house.

Kit Carson had almost forgotten the familiar smells of the cozy home and he inhaled with pleasure. His one-year-old son was sitting on a blanket spread over a corner of the room and Carson's eyes glowed. He tucked the package under his arm to pick up the child.

"Reckon this is Charles!" he said, raising the baby above his head and little Charles gurgled happily. "You was jest a red little thing the last time I saw you!"

He set the child back onto the blanket and took the package from under his arm. Teresina tried to grab it from his hand but he raised the package out of reach.

"Not this one, honey—this is fer yer mother." He handed it to Josefa. Teresina pouted as Carson sat down in a large comfortable chair and his eyes twinkled. "Now, you'll jest have t'hunt fer yers," he told the children.

Kit Junior scrambled into his father's lap and Teresina ran forward. The two began digging eagerly into Carson's coat pockets while he laughed until they finally discovered the peppermint candy, withdrawing it with cries of delight.

Josefa had opened the package and draped the brightly colored shawl over her head. "How beautiful!" she told her husband. "Just wait till they see me at the market wearing this!"

Teresina and Kit Junior sat on the floor at their father's feet and began sucking on the peppermint sticks. Josefa gave them a reproachful look.

"*Hijos*, you should wait till after supper. And also, save some candy for your brother!"

"Where is William?" Carson asked.

"He is getting firewood," Josefa replied. "He will be here soon."

She removed the shawl and placed it on a table. "Thank you for my present, *Querido*." She kissed her husband lovingly on the cheek. "Now, I will make you a nice homecoming supper."

As she went to the kitchen, the front door opened and a thin young boy of nearly twelve years entered with a load of firewood in one arm. He didn't notice his father and dropped the wood at the fireplace.

"William," Josefa called from the kitchen. "You cannot see. . .*Papa está aquí!*"

The boy's face broke into a smile and he rushed to grab his father as Carson rose from the chair. "Papa," William said. "I'm so glad to see you home again!"

Carson rumpled his son's brown hair. "Durned if you ain't grown 'bout a foot! How's that pony I got you the last time. . .you still ridin' 'im?"

William stood back with affection. "Yes, I hunt in the mountains a lot. I bring Mama rabbits and sometimes a deer!"

Carson's gray eyes filled with admiration. "You're a fine young man. I'm right proud of you."

William got the fireplace going and Teresina helped Josefa put a delicious supper on the table. Afterwards they all sat in front of the cheery fire while Kit Carson told them stories of his trapping days before coming to New Mexico. William and Teresina had heard the stories before, but they sprawled on the floor next to Kit Junior and listened in awe while Josefa cuddled little Charles in her lap. Soon, the children's interest began to lag and Teresina's eyes drooped.

"*Hora de dormir, hijos,*" Josefa said. "It is time for bed." She handed the baby to her daughter. "And here, Teresina, be sure your little brother is asleep before you get into your bed."

"*Sí, Mama.*" Teresina took the child and reluctantly followed her brothers to their room.

As they sat before the fire, Josefa gazed lovingly at her husband's face. She recalled their marriage when she was only fifteen, some eighteen years younger than her husband, and suppressed a laugh—perhaps he had married her while she was so young in order to keep some other man from claiming her.

It had been a happy union, filled with devotion and the absence of troubles. But now, Josefa felt the intrusion of sadness when she looked into her husband's eyes.

"*Querido,*" she said gently, "You have not yet told me how long you will be with us this time. . .and I have seen a dark look in your eyes ever since you arrived."

Carson took his wife's hand. "I got only two weeks and I have t'go back to Fort Stanton."

"But that is not what troubles you," she replied knowingly.

He sighed wearily. "It's jest that I've gotten myself into a corner I don't like."

"Corner?"

"With the Indians. The Army wants me to make 'em go to a reservation up near the Pecos."

"Is that so bad?"

"It's jest the way I have t'do it that's not good."

"How is that?"

"We've had t'kill some of the Apaches already, and I didn't want that to happen. I'll never forget ol' Gian-Nah-Tah's face when he told me that he and his people couldn't trust me any more. If you've ever had an old friend tell you that, you'll know how it can hurt."

Josefa looked into the crackling fire with disappointment. She wished her husband had never gone to talk with that general in Santa Fe.

"With you home, now, I thought maybe it was finished," she said, "and you could stay with us."

"No, it's only the beginnin'. When I saw General Carleton yesterday, he told me we have to start with the Navajos, now—and there's a lot more of them than the Apaches. It's gonna be a long, hard campaign, and I don't expect you'll be seein' much of me fer a spell."

Josefa leaned over to kiss her husband's cheek. "Then I think we should love each other as much as possible before you have to leave again."

Terry O'Neill spent the days at Fort Stanton, wondering what would happen to him if Kit Carson's resignation were accepted. He was both surprised and relieved when the colonel returned and asked that Terry report to the Orderly Room.

When Terry entered, the colonel was again pacing the floor with hands behind his back; Terry knew by Carson's grim look that General Carleton had talked him into remaining in the Army.

"Did you find your family in good health?" Terry asked."

"They're all fine," Carson replied.

"And how was your meeting with General Carleton? I was hoping that with the Apaches now settled at Bosque Redondo, all this turmoil would be over. But I guess he didn't accept your resignation."

"General Carleton's given me orders that when the last Mescalero

Apache has been sent to Bosque Redondo, I'm to start a campaign against the Navajos in the north," Carson said. "I'll be takin' two companies with me to Navajo country as soon as weather allows—and, with my adjutant sent back east on sick leave, I'll need you t'go along, too."

Terry's shoulders slumped at the thought of killing more Indians. He wondered, now, if he wouldn't have been better off in the east, fighting the Confederates.

"But, now, I need you to write an official order," Carson said.

Terry quickly sat down with pencil and paper. His spirits were elevated as the colonel dictated:

> "Due to the sickness of my adjutant and his transfer back east, Private Terence O'Neill of the United States Regular Army has, on this date, been promoted to Corporal and assigned as clerical assistant to Colonel Christopher Carson, Commander of First New Mexico Volunteers."

Terry looked up in astonishment. "Corporal?"

Carson harrumphed. "I'm bumpin' you up a grade. You'll be deservin' it when we start fightin' the Navajos!"

CHAPTER FOURTEEN

A soft blanket of snow covered southeastern New Mexico in December, decorating the mountains and piñons with nature's own way of heralding the Christmas season. Fort Stanton's activities slowed to almost hibernation. A handful of Indians were still camped in their stick-and-mud hovels outside the fort while the others waited for spring before coming in to surrender.

Terry's and Ben's footsteps gave a muffled crunch as they walked, huddled in their greatcoats, across the snow-covered parade ground to the mess hall. Colonel Carson had given the post cook permission to keep a large pot of hot coffee on hand during the day for anyone who came in and the hall was a popular place to stop for warmth and casual talk.

Once inside the cozy room Terry and Ben stomped the snow off their boots and noticed that only one other person was there. It was Captain Nicholas Hodt.

"Good morning, men," Hodt called from the wooden table where he sat with his coffee. "Grab your cups and join me."

Terry and Ben poured their coffee and went to the table, seating themselves across from the captain.

"I suppose you're wondering why I'm not having my coffee at the officers' mess," Hodt said. He took the familiar flask from his coat and added whiskey to the cup. "It's just that they don't look kindly on the way I take my coffee."

"Every man to his own taste," Ben said amiably.

Hodt sipped from his cup. "Well, are you boys all ready for Christmas?"

Terry shrugged. "Christmas? What's that? I feel like I'm as far away from Christmas as I'll ever get!"

Hodt gave him a gentle look. "I suppose it is hard for young men like you with families back home."

Terry had often wondered about Nicholas Hodt's background, with his smooth looks and better command of the English language.

"You mean you don't have anyone back home to think about?" Terry asked.

"Used to, but not any more," Hodt replied. "I lost my parents back east years ago. Later, I brought a pretty young bride out here, hoping to start an exciting new life." His eyes blurred slightly. "It was only a couple of months before she took sick and died. Then I joined the Army. I never had any children, of course, so you see. . .there's no one 'back home' to think about during Christmas."

Terry watched sadly as the captain poured more whiskey into his cup. Hodt caught Terry's eye.

"I never liked this stuff very much," the captain said with a rueful look at the flask. "But I've found it helps me cope with all the hell I have to put up with. You think I'm trying to forget my wife? Well, maybe I am, but it's not just her memory." He returned the flask to his coat. "It's the whole damned human race! People killing each other for no reason!" He waved his hand toward the window. "Look at all the suffering and death out there . . .those poor starving Indians waiting in the cold to be forced to walk a hundred miles across a frozen prairie, only to find another place of suffering and death! What hurts is knowing that I'm a part of the whole damned thing and there's nothing I can do about it!"

Terry and Ben sat in silence, for there was nothing they could think of to say. Captain Hodt finished his coffee and got up from the table.

"Sorry, boys," he mumbled. "I've been talking out of turn. I'd better get back to my quarters. . .maybe I can sleep this off."

Terry and Ben watched the captain weave himself out of the mess hall and disappear into the white cold outside.

"You know, Terry," Ben said, "there's a lot of truth in what he says."

Terry drank his coffee. "Well, he's right about one thing. We're all a part of it, and there's nothing we can do about it."

Ben looked at his friend seriously. "I wish I could be like you, Terry. You look death in the face like it's just another job you have to do."

"Well, how else can you handle it? Look, Ben, you're not going to change the world. You have to go along with the tide. . . otherwise, you'll just get swept under!"

When they got back to the tent, Terry wrote a letter to his parents hoping they had a nice Christmas, for he knew it would be months before they would see his words. Then he began a letter to Susan Godfrey.

"Maybe by writing to you," he told her, "and thinking of all the wonderful times we had together during this time of year, I can forget about the loneliness out here in this strange land and all the unpleasant things taking place around me. I look forward to the time when I can leave all this behind and live again in a civilized world."

CHAPTER FIFTEEN

Deacon and Moony were put in charge of a group of Apaches who were ordered to work on Fort Sumner's construction but it was difficult, for the Indians were constantly weak from hunger and accomplished little. Agent Labadie went again to talk with Commander Updegraff.

"They used up their last rations two days ago," Labadie complained, "and it'll be two more days before more arrive! I beg of you to allow some of them to go out and hunt for wild game. It's the only way to keep them from starving!"

"But if we let them go, they'll escape and go back to their own land," the commander argued.

"Not if they leave their wives and children behind as hostages."

Captain John Cremony, who had lived with the Apaches and spoke their language, was assigned to take a party out hunting.

"We can't let them carry guns," Cremony told Updegraff, "only their bows and arrows. And, to show my trust in them, I won't carry a gun, either."

Updegraff was shocked. "Why, they'll get you alone out there and kill you!"

"If I show I trust them, they'll trust me," Cremony said, then smiled ruefully. "But I'll hide a Bowie knife and four pistols in my coat, just in case."

The hunting party was a great success; they returned with a large number of killed antelope and the Indians finally were given some nourishment.

Labadie had kinder words for the post commander when they next spoke. "Even without the government's support, the Apaches have improved their homes."

"Now that they've been settled at Bosque Redondo," Updegraff said, "I have orders from General Carleton to get them started on their farms."

Labadie frowned. "Obviously, the general hasn't reckoned with the Apache disposition. They're nomads—it would be an insult for them to work in the fields."

Updegraff smirked. "And you haven't reckoned with General Carleton.

When he orders the Apaches to start farming, it's my duty to see that they do so!"

With Labadie's help and supervision of the soldiers, the Apaches reluctantly started working. Proper farm tools had not arrived, so the Indians were forced to work with their bare hands, digging irrigation ditches and planting over two hundred acres in corn, beans and melons.

Deacon Jones and Moony Calhoun sat under a warm spring sun, rifles slung on their shoulders, and watched the Indians toiling in the fields.

"I bet them pore Indians'll starve to death before their crops ever git ripe enough to eat," Deacon said lazily.

"I don't think they're plannin' to wait," Moony replied. "I heard some of 'em escaped durin' the night and went back to their own country."

"Well, I can't blame 'em—they never get enough food in this danged Bosque Redondo."

"I don't know what I was thinkin' about when I volunteered to come out here!" Moony said. "So far, this here fort's only a couple of buildings and we're still livin' in tents!"

"And when I joined the Army, I never thought I'd be kickin' an Indian's butt. I hear there's a bunch more of them Apaches arrivin' next week."

Deacon gave a longing sigh. "Wonder what it'd take t'get 'em to send us back to Fort Stanton?!"

CHAPTER SIXTEEN

The fresh smell of pine and piñon spread over Fort Stanton as Terry read another message from General Carleton.

"Now, with good weather, you are to prepare immediately for our campaign against the Navajos. Select ten Ute Indians as scouts and four of the best Mexican guides you can find. Take two companies from Fort Stanton and proceed to Fort Wingate where you will take on another three hundred men. I want you to eventually have a force of at least seven hundred to enter Navajo country.

"Never lax the use of force with a people that can no more be trusted than the wolves that run through the mountains. All Navajos who desire peace will be considered 'good' Navajos and sent to Bosque Redondo. They will have until July 20 to surrender. After that, every Navajo will be considered hostile and treated accordingly. I will be waiting for word of your progress in this campaign."

Terry and Ben were among the two companies that left Fort Stanton with Colonel Kit Carson in the heat of early July, moving north across rugged Malpais—the "Bad Country" of hardened lava that had spewed thousands of years ago from nearby Mount Taylor.

The tired group finally arrived at Fort Wingate on a hot afternoon where Kit Carson would be acting post commander during a three-day rest. Another three hundred and twenty-six men waited to join them.

The soldiers staggered to their barracks and collapsed onto the straw mattresses, a welcome relief to the hard ground they had been sleeping on during the last ten days.

"I've had a ache in my gut ever since we left," Snake Eater complained. "Wonder if there's anything that'd make me feel better?"

Grizzly Taylor gave him a sneering laugh. "Ain't no wonder, with all them snakes in yer belly!"

"If you ever ate one," Snake Eater shot back, "you wouldn't have to kill it first!"

Dakota Williams lay back dreamily. "The only thing that'd make me feel good right now is a good shot o' whiskey!"

"Maybe some molasses would help your stomach," Ben Adams told Snake Eater. "That's what my Ma always gave me back on the farm whenever I had a bellyache."

"Why don't you come with me," Terry told Snake Eater. "I have to report to the colonel. I'll write a request for you to buy some molasses at the sutler's and we'll have Colonel Carson sign it."

Four men were in Carson's quarters, rehashing old times, when Terry and Snake Eater arrived. Terry went in while Snake Eater waited by the outside door.

"Thanks fer reportin' so soon," Carson greeted Terry. "Come in and meet some tough old cronies o' mine!"

Terry was introduced to Major Joseph Cummings, a short rugged man with a black moustache, and two captains, John Thompson and Jacob Riley. The latter two stood tall with dark blond hair and faint moustaches. None of them would be taken for officers in their boots and buckskin trousers, except, maybe, for the blue army coat hanging casually open. All three were a good ten years younger than Kit Carson.

"These scoundrels helped me fight off the Confederates at Valverde seven years ago," Carson said with pride. "Now, they're gonna help me round up them Navajos."

Terry and the men acknowledged introductions and Terry felt he had come at a bad time. "I can come back later, if you want me to," Terry said to Carson.

"Oh, no," Carson replied. "Gotta send a message to General Carleton, tellin' him we got here all right. You know what to say, so why don't you jest set down over there and write it up fer me."

"Before we get started," Terry said, "Private Simmons is waiting outside. . .he has a little stomach trouble. I've written a request for him to buy some molasses, if you'd be so kind to sign it for him." He handed the request to the colonel.

Carson glanced over the paper and looked up at Terry, as if for clarification.

"Yes, it's in order," Terry confirmed.

The colonel signed it and gave the request back to Terry. "Hope this helps," Carson said. "I want my men in good shape t'leave in three days. Anybody else needs somethin' jest let me know."

Terry stepped outside and gave the request to Snake Eater, then returned to the room and wrote the letter to General Carleton.

After Snake Eater got his molasses from the sutler, he returned to the barracks.

"You know," he told the other men, "I don't think the colonel can read. I watched through the door while he had to have O'Neill tell him what that request said."

Dakota Williams thought a moment. "Maybe I can get some whiskey, after all. If the colonel cain't read, I'll write a request for a canteen of whiskey and tell him it's fer molasses."

"Yeah," Grizzly Taylor said, "an' what if he *can* read? You'll spend the rest of yer time here in the guardhouse!"

Dakota waited until Terry had come back to the barracks. Knowing that Colonel Carson wouldn't have anyone to read for him, Dakota took his request for whiskey to be signed by the commander.

"There's been a run of this stomach trouble in our company," Dakota told the colonel, "and that molasses seems to help. If you'd sign this request, I'd sure be obliged."

Kit Carson looked at the paper and then signed it. "You men take care of yerselves," he said and gave it back to Dakota.

The next day, not only did Snake Eater and Dakota return to Kit Carson with another order for "molasses," but Grizzly Taylor and another man showed up with their own requests and the colonel signed them, hoping that the strange sickness would be taken care of.

On their last day at the fort, Kit Carson visited the sutler's store to check on the supplies he would need for the campaign.

"Well, John," Carson asked John Waters, the sutler, "how's business?"

"Kinda brisk on whiskey," John Waters replied. "Sold a barrel full in just the last two days!"

Carson was taken aback. "John, don't you know that it's agin regulations t'sell whiskey to enlisted men without a written order from the commanding officer?"

"Why, yes," Waters replied in surprise. "Every sale has been made on your signed order. Here, come and see."

The sutler walked behind the counter and shoved forward his order ring, which was a wire set in a block of wood. There were six orders stuck on it. "All of them here are signed by Colonel Kit Carson!" John Waters said.

Later that day, Terry had to control his laughter when the colonel told him of the episode.

"From now on," Kit Carson said with chagrin, "I ain't signin' nothin' till somebody else reads it first!"

Chapter Seventeen

Kit Carson left Fort Wingate with over five hundred men in his command, riding northwest across the hot flatlands. Purple mountains rested miles away, but the distance was misleading and Terry thought it shouldn't be long before they reached the abandoned Fort Defiance in Arizona territory where Carson planned to make his headquarters.

As they rode along in the hot sun, Ben spotted a column of dark smoke rising against the soft blue sky.

"Wonder what's burnin'?" he thought aloud.

"Maybe it's Indians," Terry replied.

He looked to see Kit Carson's reaction, but the colonel kept riding unconcerned and Terry thought he must be able to tell Indian smoke from any other kind.

They eventually rode over the hill to find a small house and corral nestled at the bottom. Smoke was drifting lazily out through a window and open door. There was no sign of life and Carson led his men down to the area where he called the company to a halt. After Carson and Major Cummings dismounted and walked to the corral, Terry saw what Kit Carson had spotted long before any of the others.

A young woman sat on the ground with her skirt spread around her legs. She held a tiny baby in her arms, rocking it gently, while staring at a man who lay on his back in front of her. Not only was there was an arrow in his chest, but his face had been crushed to an unrecognizable mass of blood and bones. A large blood-stained rock lay nearby with remnants of brain matter clinging to its surface.

"Navajos?" Major Cummings asked the colonel.

Carson nodded. "They're the only ones who bash their enemy's head in to make sure he's dead."

The woman had never taken her eyes from the dead man and Carson squatted down beside her.

"I'm Colonel Carson, New Mexico Volunteers, ma'am," he said gently. "Is this here your husband?"

She kept staring at the body and nodded while still rocking the baby.

"I'm sorry," Carson said. "What's your name, ma'am?"

She took a moment to answer. "Farrow. . .Ellen Farrow."

Carson looked over at the corral. All of the logs on one side were broken down and the pen was empty.

"I'm sorry, too, they burned out your house and took your cattle. Do you have anyplace t'go to, now?"

She only shook her head.

"Well, ma'am, we cain't jest leave you and your baby here by yourselves."

She finally looked up at him. "A sister. I have a sister in Albuquerque."

"You know how to find her?"

"Yes. I used to live there with her and her husband."

Carson took her arm. "Well, come now, Mrs. Farrow, we'll give your husband a proper burial, then a couple o' my men will take you back to yer sister."

He helped the woman to her feet and she looked at the large company of men. Her face wrinkled in anguish and she hugged the baby tightly.

"Why couldn't you have come earlier?!" she cried

Kit Carson put an arm around her until the sobs turned to sniffles. He turned to Major Cummings. "I want you t'help Mrs. Farrow, here, git her things together, then have two men take her to Albuquerque. They can catch up with us at Fort Defiance."

Terry's feelings for the Indians were in turmoil, now. He had begun to feel a small compassion for them, but here was an example of what terrible things they were capable of doing. His heart went out to the poor Mrs. Farrow whose husband had been so brutally murdered.

CHAPTER EIGHTEEN

Willow-In-Storm sat among the sweet-smelling piñon and tall ponderosas, watching sadly as her sheep grazed on a small area of grass. It was getting harder each day to find enough forage for the animals and half of them had already died. Her people had eaten the animals right away, for there was little food for them, as well; she wondered what they would do when all the sheep were gone.

Willow-In-Storm saw that the distant mountains were casting long shadows and she began herding the sheep back to the village, anxious to check on her father who had become ill during the arduous trip north. He was resting his frail body next to the small fire when she entered the hogan.

"I was able to find some piñon nuts and berries on the way home," she told her father. "They will go well with the little corn we have."

The elderly man gazed at his daughter with bleary eyes. "I know there is not enough for everyone," he said. "Feed the children first. . .if any food is left, then I will eat."

She stroked his long white hair. "The children are strong and can do with little. You are weak and need something in your stomach."

The door flap raised and Standing Bear came into the hogan. "I have killed a squirrel," he said, holding up the dead animal. "It is for you and your father to eat."

Willow-In-Storm was pleased. "There will be enough for all. Sit with your brother and I will prepare your food."

Standing Bear squatted down next to his brother.

"Our scouts have been hiding among the boulders, watching the white man's army move deeper into Dinetah," Standing Bear said. "There are many soldiers and they have already destroyed two of our people's farms and killed their cattle."

Willow-In-Storm paused while preparing the squirrel. "What will we do? Our people are hungry and the sheep and horses are dying. . .in not long we will have nothing!"

Her uncle shook his head. "If we stay here, they will find us. I think we should keep moving north to the big canyon *Tseghi*. There, the high walls will protect us."

"But your brother is too ill to travel," Willow-In-Storm argued.

Her father raised a shaky hand. "Standing Bear is the wise one. If he thinks we should go, then we must go."

The Indians packed their belongings once more to begin another hard journey. Willow-In-Storm carefully bundled her father onto a travois that was pulled by one of the healthier horses and she walked along beside him. The sheep were left behind, for it was decided they were too weak and wouldn't find enough grass to sustain them during the trip.

The group moved slowly, struggling against the rocky inclines and thin air of higher elevation, while the rough ground, studded with jagged debris, was not kind to Willow-In-Storm's father. She stopped the horse often to let him rest with a sip of water from the goat skin carried on her shoulder.

When they finally reached the mountainous canyon, its deep red and yellow vertical cliffs spread huge shadows over a small yellow valley on the west where the rusty-red arch of Window Rock sat like a frame against a dark-blue sky.

They chose an area in one of the many small canyons running off from the large one and began scrounging material to build their fork-stick hogans. There was enough scrub oak available to build fires and Willow-In-Storm warmed a soup of berries and roots to give her ailing father.

"I am very worried," Willow-In-Storm told her uncle. "Your brother eats little, there is no color in his face and his forehead carries the heat of a stone lying in the sun."

The Singer was called and the old medicine man began the Trembling Hand ceremony. Willow-In-Storm sat with her uncle in the darkness watching while the Singer moved shaking hands over her father's body and uttered the familiar chants. Tired and hungry, she soon fell asleep on her uncle's lap.

It was early morning when Standing Bear placed a hand on his niece's shoulder and she awoke to see him looking down with a sad face. The Singer was no longer in the hogan and a terrible sadness cut through her heart.

"Your father is now with the sun, clouds and air we breathe," Standing Bear said and took her hand. "Come, we must leave, for Chindi has visited this house."

She followed him outside and they stood breathing in the crisp morning air. Willow-In-Storm knew that death was only the end of one's life cycle, but the loss of her father still brought tears to her eyes.

"Now that the god of death has passed through this house," Standing

Bear said, "you cannot enter it again. The hogan must be destroyed. You will come live with me."

Willow-In-Storm wiped her damp cheeks. "I am old enough not to be a burden on you. . .I can build another house."

Her uncle smiled ruefully. "My offer has two sides. Until a brave takes you for his wife, you need someone to look after you, and I am getting old. I think we need to help each other."

Willow-In-Storm realized he was right, for now, she felt alone and helpless.

"You speak wisely," she said. "It is what my father would wish."

CHAPTER NINETEEN

The large army of men, horses and pack mules arrived at Fort Defiance, in the Arizona territory, only to find the place in near ruins. Kit Carson ordered the soldiers to pitch tents for accommodations and then he dictated a message to General Carleton:

"Fort Defiance has been nearly destroyed by the Navajos who hate the white men's desecratin' their sacred land," Carson said. "Therefore, I request your allowin' me to build another fort in this same area fer my headquarters. With your permission, I'll call it Fort Canby, since Colonel Edward Canby was the first one t'think of a reservation fer the Navajos."

After the general's quick approval, the men worked fast in good weather on the construction of Fort Canby while Kit Carson sent out parties in search of Indians. The soldiers were unaware of the Navajos watching from their hiding places as the white men spread through hills and canyons like hungry ants.

Terry O'Neill remained at Fort Canby with Colonel Carson while Ben Adams and the others went out with the first unit, under command of Captain John Thompson. They rode all morning without seeing any sign of Indians and soon came to Navajo farmland where a large field of golden wheat shimmered in the sun.

"Let the horses eat their fill here," Captain Thompson ordered, "then trample and burn what's left!"

Ben Adams saw a group of hogans at the edge of the field.
"What about the Indians, sir," he asked warily and fingered the trigger of his rifle. "They might come out fightin'!"

"No need to worry," the captain replied, squinting toward the tiny settlement. "They've seen us coming and run off. Besides, we're too many for them."

After the horses had eaten, Ben joined a group of soldiers setting fire to the wheat field and watched it go up in billows of gray smoke. Then they loped over to the Indian homes.

"All right, men," Captain Thompson said, "put a torch to all these hogans and burn 'em out!"

Grizzly Taylor lit a handful of straw and, with an excited yelp, threw it into a hogan. Ben and Snake Eater joined the others in setting the meager homes on fire, then sat on their horses, watching, as the Navajos' last possessions vanished in ugly orange flames and black smoke.

Captain Thompson's party continued riding through the hills until late afternoon when they found another small farm where the Navajos had fled at the sight of approaching soldiers. More crops were destroyed while Ben, Grizzly, Snake Eater and Dakota rode over to the hogans, putting torches to the homes.

An old woman with long gray hair and clad in only a threadbare dress hobbled out of one of the huts. She raised a bony arm to the sky and her rheumy eyes glared at the white soldiers.

"You will die!" she told them loudly. "When the sun is straight overhead, you will all die!"

Grizzly Taylor laughed. "This old hag must be a witch. . . let's take care of her!"

Ben tried to intervene. "We're supposed to take all the women prisoners!"

Grizzly ignored him and got down from his horse. He drew a large knife while Ben remained in the saddle, wondering what kind of devilment Grizzly was up to.

The heavy black-bearded man stepped slowly around the woman, holding his knife outstretched.

"I hear tell you Indian witches hide medicine bags under yer clothes," he said. "Come on, Granny, let's see if you got any on you!"

Grizzly whipped the knife toward the woman, ripping part of the dress from her shoulder while Snake Eater and Dakota dismounted with excited grins. They drew their knives, also.

"Show us, old woman!" Snake Eater yelped and slashed at the woman's other shoulder. The dress fell to her waist and she stood rooted to the ground with angry eyes.

Ben had seen enough. "All right," he shouted. "Leave her alone and let's go on!"

The men ignored Ben's protest and danced around the old Navajo, slashing at her until the dress had been cut away, exposing her naked wrinkled body.

"Lookee there!" Grizzly shouted. "She's got bags o' magic powder tied on her—don't nobody touch 'em!"

He cut two small leather pouches from the woman's waist and carried them on the blade of his knife to a burning hogan, then threw them into the flames.

"Come on," Ben shouted again, "you've had your fun. Now, let's get on with the others!"

Grizzly drew his pistol and walked over to the old woman while she stared at him resolutely. He put the gun to her head and fired.

"God damn you!" Ben screamed.

The men got back on their horses and rode off, laughing. Ben sat for a moment, looking with frustration at the dead woman whose brains were splattered around her shattered head. Reflections of the furiously burning hogans danced wickedly on a quickening pool of blood and Ben's stomach wrenched. He quickly wheeled the horse around to join the others.

As the company of soldiers returned from their forays, Ben wondered if perhaps there had been other old or sick Navajos in the hogans when they were set on fire. He shuddered and the old Indian woman's threatening words played in his mind all the way back to the fort.

When Ben Adams dragged himself, tired and dirty, into the tent Terry smiled in relief, glad to see his friend had safely returned.

"How did it go?" Terry asked. "Did you find any Indians?"

Ben sat down wearily on his cot. "Only an old woman. . .all the others had run away."

Terry was glad for him. "Then you didn't have to do any killing."

Ben looked up and the whites of his eyes seemed to bore out of his dirty face. "They killed the old woman."

"But women and children are to be taken captive."

"This one was a witch, so they thought she oughta be killed."

"A witch?!"

"She had these two little bags of magic powder tied on her waist." A strange look came into Ben's eyes. "She told us we'd all die when the sun was straight overhead. Reckon she meant exactly noon."

After the evening meal, Kit Carson asked Terry to come to his quarters and read Captain Thompson's written report on the day's mission. Terry quoted all the details of Navajo crops and houses that were destroyed, with one old woman killed. When he finished, he studied Kit Carson's face to see if there was any indication of his thoughts on the matter, but the colonel's expression hadn't changed.

"If we keep burning them out like this," Terry said, "the Indians will starve without their crops. . .and when winter comes, they'll freeze without their homes."

"Well, it's better than fightin' 'em with the barrel of a gun," Carson said. "It wouldn't happen if they'd jest surrender and go to the Bosque."

Terry shook his head in confusion. "It just seems there should be some other way of handling it!"

The colonel noted Terry's pained face and said gruffly, "Then I wonder jest how you would do it?" He walked angrily out of the room.

Terry wrote two more letters that night. He never dwelt on the unpleasant side of his activities when he wrote to his parents, for he didn't want to upset them. However, Susan had always understood his feelings and offered constructive suggestions. He had told her previously of his admiration for Colonel Kit Carson, but now he had another view.

"Each day I find my faith in human nature being shaken," he wrote. "Now, the man whom I had looked up to is like a statue on a crumbling pedestal. I'm unable to cope with all the terrible events that are slowly chipping away at my respect for Colonel Kit Carson."

CHAPTER TWENTY

"I am discouraged at the ineffective progress of our campaign against the Navajos," General Carleton said in his latest message as Terry read it to Kit Carson. "To date, not one Navajo has been delivered to Bosque Redondo. I must impress upon you to step up your pursuit of the Indians. Make them know that they must surrender or you will kill them!"

For a greater show of force, Carleton ordered another two hundred military personnel sent to Fort Canby and Kit Carson sent out several scouting parties in all directions.

Now Carson, himself, was leading two companies, one in his command and the other one under Major Joseph Cummings. Terry O'Neill rode with Kit Carson while Ben Adams, Grizzly, Dakota and Snake Eater went with Major Cummings and his men.

The two units soon came upon a small group of Navajo hogans surrounding a tiny wheat field. Smoke still curled up from the fires and it was obvious that the Indians had fled only moments before, upon seeing the white men approach. Terry noticed an Indian child, perhaps five years old, standing beside the door of one hogan.

"That little boy," Terry said to Kit Carson, "he must have been left behind when everybody ran away."

Carson studied the child who gazed with wondering black eyes at the strange white men. "We'll have to take him with us."

"But his folks," Terry worried, "they'll come back for him, won't they?"

"They'll keep hidin' out fer weeks, or even longer. The boy'll starve to death if we leave 'im here." He turned to the company. "One o' you men let that little Indian boy ride behind you and let's keep movin'.'"

When they rode away, Terry thought of some poor Navajo mother who was no doubt crying for the little son she would never see again.

As the Army units neared a small canyon, a large group of Navajos was spotted in the distance and the two groups split up, hoping to surround the Indians. The Navajos, however had seen the white men approach and began disappearing. Terry thought it was uncanny how the Indians could shinny up the steep canyon walls and seem to melt into the rusty stone colors.

"A lot of 'em live in the canyons," Kit Carson said, "and runnin' around on those rocks comes easy. If you can't see 'em, don't waste yer ammunition. But remember, they can still see you, so be careful!"

Major Cummings had led his company around to the other end of the short canyon but still couldn't spot any Indians.

"Stay here and keep your eyes open," he ordered his men. "If you see one of those redskins, get 'im!"

The major then dismounted and started for the canyon wall.

"Sir!" Ben Adams called. "Don't you think you oughta have a cover? It ain't safe to go in there alone!"

The major waved him away and continued toward the steep rocks. As he arrived at the base a gunshot echoed eerily through the ravine, and Major Cummings grabbed his stomach. Ben and the others quickly raised their rifles as Cummings fall to his knees. The soldiers scanned the towering rock face in a frantic search for something to shoot at, but it was like a ghost had fired the bullet.

"Come on," Ben said, "we have to get the major!"

He dismounted while Grizzly, Dakota and Snake Eater joined him. They ran over to Cummings who was lying at the foot of the cliff, unconscious and bleeding profusely.

Each man had taken hold of an arm or leg to carry the major away when a rumbling sound caught their ears. They looked up in terror as an avalanche of boulders and rocks came roaring down the canyon wall so fast they were unable to escape.

Grizzly was the first to be engulfed, then Dakota and Snake Eater also became victims beneath the crushing tonnage of rock. Ben stumbled backward and was flattened by a huge boulder that rolled onto his chest like a deadly giant's foot, pinning him down against the hard rubble.

Kit Carson and his company, having heard the sound of gunfire and crashing rocks, galloped over to find the men of Major Cummings' company sifting among the debris.

"What happened here?" Carson yelled.

"Major Cummings was shot," one of the men told him. "Four of the men tried to help and the Indians rolled rocks down on 'em!"

Terry ran his eyes over the soldiers' faces and didn't see Ben Adams; his heart grew cold. Kit Carson uttered a grumble, then got off his horse and walked over to the fallen rocks where he knelt beside Major Cummings' body.

Terry quickly dismounted to search for Ben. A wisp of bright red hair fluttered among the rubble and Terry ran over, dropping to his knees. Ben's eyes slowly opened to see his friend peering down.

"Ben!" Terry said. "Just hold on!" He turned to the others and shouted, "This man's still alive! Somebody help me dig him out!"

Ben gasped for air, wincing in pain at the effort. "If I was a horse, you'd shoot me!" he whispered.

Two men came over and helped Terry roll away the boulder. Ben uttered a groan and stiffened. Terry looked at the crushed body and knew that even with a doctor, it was hopeless. He smoothed the red hair away from Ben's eyes.

"Don't worry, Ben, we'll get you back to the fort and you'll be all right."

"It's no good," Ben choked through the blood in his mouth. "Ain't none of us can live forever."

"Don't say that, dammit!" Tears rolled down Terry's cheeks.

Ben squinted at the sky. "Look," he said weakly. "It's noon. . .the sun's straight overhead!" Then his eyes glazed over and there was no more breath in him.

CHAPTER TWENTY-ONE

Deacon Jones and Moony Calhoun were becoming more despondent, for conditions at Bosque Redondo had not improved and the major problem at the moment was drunkenness among the Indians.

"Where the hell did they get ahold of whiskey?" Moony asked in surprise.

"Ain't you ever heard of *tiswin*?" Deacon replied. "That's their kind of whiskey. They make it outta corn."

When the corn ripened, Apaches had sneaked into the fields at night and stolen enough ears to make their alcoholic drink. Now, so many of them were drunk, there were only a few who could lift a hoe or dig the irrigation ditches.

"If I had to live in this dung hole like they do," Moony said, "I'd stay drunk, too!"

"No wonder a lot of 'em escaped t'go back to their own country," Deacon added and then laughed. "When the Army went after 'em, they couldn't find a single track. Them Indians know how t'fool the white man, all right!"

"Well, maybe they'll finally do somethin' about this mess," Deacon said. "I hear the Superintendent of Indian Affairs was here yesterday. He thinks the same as me. . .this place stinks! The post commander told him the Navajos were comin' in, too, and the superintendent said he was gonna complain to that General Carleton."

Superintendent of Indian Affairs, Dr. Michael Steck, was a tall man in his early thirties. He did not sport the customary moustache, but a soft dark beard ran from one sideburn, down around the chin and up to meet the other sideburn, framing his kind face and determined eyes.

The superintendent was liked and trusted by both the Apaches and Navajos, for he did all he could, under the stultifying hand of government hierarchy, to help the Indians. Now, as he arrived in Santa Fe to confront General Carleton with the deplorable conditions at Bosque Redondo, Michael Steck's usual patience was running thin.

Carleton had already heard of Steck's disapproval of the Bosque and shook the superintendent's hand with an artificial smile.

"The Bosque is still trying to get on its feet," Carleton said amiably. "It just takes a little time."

Michael Steck sat down in the chair facing Carleton's desk. "The most urgent problem is food," he said grimly. "The Department of Indian Affairs does not have sufficient funds to help you feed the Apaches at Bosque Redondo. Since these people are being treated like prisoners of war, it should be the War Department's responsibility to take care of them."

General Carleton seated himself behind the desk and his smile quickly vanished. "This is being considered in Washington," he replied, "but these are Indians we are dealing with and Washington considers it a problem for Indian Affairs."

Steck continued. "Also, Fort Sumner's post commander informs me that soon the Navajos will start arriving. There are thousands more Navajos than Apaches—just where will the food come from?!"

"I admit we have a problem getting our rations," the general retorted, "but I assure you it will improve."

Steck was not to be dissuaded. "Also, the Apaches and Navajos are enemies, and when you put them together, you're sure to have trouble. I propose that you keep only the Apaches at the Bosque, but leave the Navajos on a reservation in their own country where they can hunt for food and grow their crops as they have been doing for hundreds of years."

Carleton realized he had another adversary sitting in front of him. "If they stay in their own country, they'll continue marauding and killing the white settlers." He glared defiantly. "Now, I have planned this whole thing and I'm determined to make it work. It will all go well only if I have the cooperation of not only the War Department, but also your Department of Indian Affairs!"

Steck rose from his chair in angry frustration. "I must remind you again, General, that my department's funds are inadequate to do so!"

All formalities had been wiped away and now, what was visible through the dense whiskers on Carleton's face turned red. "Very well," he said evenly, "I will ask that only the War Department be responsible for Bosque Redondo. . .but the Navajos will still be quartered there!"

Michael Steck bade the general farewell, without shaking his hand, and could see nothing but disaster in Carleton's plan, for he knew legislature in Washington was blind to the problem. He decided to go to Washington himself and make a full report to Commissioner Dole.

CHAPTER TWENTY-TWO

Colonel Kit Carson and his men returned to Fort Canby in dejection, since they had little to show for their efforts. Terry O'Neill also came back with a heavy heart, but it was for the loss of his good friend Ben Adams who was buried with the others in the hills of this beautiful but angry land.

Terry's spirits were lightened when he found three of Susan Godfrey's letters waiting. It took months for mail to get back and forth, especially with Terry's changes of address, and when letters did arrive it was almost like Christmas. He read Susan's letters twice and ached to be away from this depressing world and back in her arms again.

Kit Carson's return was not so pleasant. He found that conditions at Fort Canby had gone wildly out of control in the hands of the acting post commander Major Thomas Blakeney. Carson heard the bad news, first hand, from his loyal friend Captain Asa Carey.

"Pardon my being frank," Captain Carey said, "and it's just between us, but Major Blakeney is a complete ass! He is self-centered and overbearing. He does not discipline the troops and lets them have as much whiskey as they want. He permits whores to come and go as they please and, what's more deplorable, the officer of the day was found drunk and in bed with an enlisted man!"

Kit Carson soaked in the information with a firm jaw. "And what's this I hear about some Indians bein' killed?" he asked.

Captain Carey took a breath and continued. "Major Blakeney has a death wish for Indians. Four Navajos arrived several days ago to talk peace. Blakeney had them seized and dragged off to prison. One old man was shot, supposedly while trying to escape. The other Indians were forced to clean the parade ground, burying dead dogs and feces with their bare hands. Two eventually escaped but were hunted down and murdered!"

"I thank you fer givin' me the honest facts in this matter," Carson said. "I'll report Major Blakeney's actions and have him replaced." Then he looked Captain Carey in the eyes. "I've always been able to rely on you. . .and you know how to treat the Indians right. I think it'd be a good idea fer you to take command of this fort while I'm away."

Charges were pressed against Major Blakeney, but Carson was perturbed to learn that the complaints were quickly dropped since Blakeney was a good friend of General James Carleton.

Another impatient message from Carleton arrived and Terry O'Neill read it for Kit Carson:

"So far, you have captured only a few Navajos. I am now issuing orders for you to immediately scout through their stronghold in Canyon de Chelly and get them started for Bosque Redondo as soon as possible."

Kit Carson pulled at his moustache and Terry could see that the colonel was troubled by Carleton's displeasure.

"This is a bad time o' year to go trampin' through Canyon de Chelly," Carson muttered. "With winter comin' on it'll be durned hard on both the horses and the men. Plus the fact that it'll be next to impossible to ferret out them Navajos livin' in caves high up on the canyon walls."

The steep walls of Canyon de Chelly soared nearly two thousand feet high in places, with offshoot canyons that opened onto beautiful savannas where the Navajos cultivated grain and orchards.

Kit Carson took three companies north in sweeping cold winds and split them up to ride through the various canyons, destroying fields of grain and cutting down the Navajos' groves of peach trees.

While riding through a canyon with the Kit Carson company, Terry noticed the sky changing from pale blue to a deep purple.

"Looks like we're in for a blue norther," one of the soldiers remarked.

"What's a blue norther?" Terry asked as he studied the strange phenomenon.

"Temperature can drop fifty degrees in five minutes or less! Up in the Texas Panhandle, when one o' these things came along, I seen cattle grazin' in the sun one minute and freezin' to death the next!"

Not far away, Captain Jacob Riley's company arrived at a wide area in one of the small canyons where a fruit grove stood. The nearby hogans had been deserted and Riley ordered his men to halt.

"All right, everybody," he said, "let's take our axes and cut these trees down."

The captain didn't use rank as an excuse and joined his men in the task. They tethered their horses at the edge of the grove and began swinging axes at the tree trunks. The work soon brought out a good sweat and the men took off their shirts to continue chopping down trees while the sky began turning an ominous purple.

Captain Riley noticed a chill in the air and looked up at the fading sun.

"Looks like we're in for cold weather. Get a move on. . .we're almost finished!"

One of the men dropped his axe and shivered. "Dammit," he grumbled, "I'm gonna go git my coat!" He put on his shirt and started to go back where the horses had been tethered, but stopped in astonishment.

"They're gone!" he yelled. "Look. . .all of our horses are gone!"

The men stopped working and gaped in disbelief.

"Damned Indians stole 'em!" one of them said. "And our coats, too!"

Captain Riley's heart sank. All their food and water had vanished as well. He looked again at the threatening sky and shuddered as a gust of icy wind raced through the canyon.

Snow had already begun to fall in the area where Kit Carson and his company were traveling. It was late in the day, so he ordered his men to halt and make camp on the spot.

They built a fire to cook a warm supper and later old timers in the company gave pointers to the others as they bedded down for the night.

For warmth, two men slept together with two blankets spread on the ground and their two greatcoats placed on top. This was covered with two more blankets to sleep under. Each man would then have a dry blanket in the morning to put next to his horse, with the damp blanket next to the saddle.

As the men huddled against each other, the falling snow that covered them added even more warmth. After an exhausting ride, it was not long before the entire company was fast asleep.

In the adjacent canyon, Captain Riley knew the only hope for his company was to hike back to find Kit Carson's group, but night was falling and Riley would have to wait till morning to start out. They were all without coats and snow was already blanketing the ground as the men huddled together in misery.

"We'll have to make it through the night the best we can," he told his freezing men. "Take those axes and dig holes before the snow gets too deep. Two men will sleep together in each hole to keep warm. Cut down tree branches to cover yourselves!"

The men huddled next to each other in the holes, unable to sleep with the snow and freezing wind blowing over them. Captain Riley was relieved to find next morning that the blizzard had passed and, thankfully, no one had frozen to death. However, the most grueling hazard was yet to come; they would have to find Colonel Carson's group before it started moving on.

There was no way to build a fire and Riley prayed that they could survive a treacherous march through the freezing canyon. He gathered the men together and they began walking, with arms wrapped around their bodies and teeth chattering.

They came to a stream that was frozen over, but the ice was too thin to walk across. Captain Riley broke through and waded in the icy water as the others followed. When they reached the other side, their legs and feet had lost all feeling and it was difficult to move them forward through the heavy drifts of snow.

Hours passed while some of the soldiers dropped to their knees with faces covered by a mask of white frost. Others helped them to their feet and they pushed themselves through the deep snowdrifts, gasping for breath. Captain Riley tried to keep the men together, but the line became stretched to a point where it was every man for himself.

A light wind came up, chilling their bodies with a sub-zero cold so numbing that their minds gave way and several ambled off in all directions, sobbing in despair. Those who dropped into the snow were left to freeze to death while the others staggered onward.

At the Carson camp, Terry pushed his face up through the snow in the morning light. As he looked around, it seemed that he was alone with a mantle of white covering everything. One by one, the soldiers emerged from the snow, like dead rising from the grave, and began cutting tree limbs for a fire. The wood was still wet and it took some time before the men were able to boil coffee and heat their breakfast.

Later, while getting their horses ready to continue the ride, Terry thought he heard a faint cry for help in the quiet chilly air. He was not alone, for everyone stopped what they were doing and listened as another plaintive shout was heard.

"Maybe it's an Indian trick," one of the men said. "They're tryin' to lead us into an ambush!"

Kit Carson turned his head in all directions, his keen ears trying to determine where the call was coming from. Echoes in the canyon were deceiving.

"You, there," he said to a capable-looking young man, "climb up to that ledge over there and look south. See if you can spot anybody."

The man did as ordered and shinnied up the steep wall of rock. He shaded his eyes from the perch and in a moment called down.

"There's a line of men way off yonder," he shouted. "Don't look like no Indians, neither!"

Carson got onto his horse and ordered three men to follow. They rode out of camp, going south, with their rifles loaded and ready while Terry and the others wondered what the colonel would find.

When Kit Carson saw Captain Riley's party, their faces were so encrusted with frost that Carson had to squint to recognize them.

"Jake!" Carson said. "What the hell happened to your horses?!"

Jacob Riley's answer came as a rasp from his frozen throat. "Indians. . . stole 'em. Took our coats. . ." Then he collapsed into the snow.

Carson turned to his mounted soldiers. "Quick, git these men on your horses and take 'em back to camp!"

It was some time before Carson and the soldiers returned, with a man sitting behind the saddle of each rider. They reined to a stop beside the dead campfire.

"Git that fire goin' agin," Carson ordered, "and make it a big one!"

The frozen men were helped down from the horses and dragged over to the campfire while it was being rekindled. Then Carson had more soldiers go back with him, leading several horses behind them to bring in the remaining survivors.

Out of a company of fifty, only Captain Riley and forty of his men were found. Three were already frozen to death like stiff bleached mummies, while the living were quickly wrapped in blankets and given hot coffee.

Terry and the others worked most of the day, rubbing the victim's frozen arms and legs, trying to force blood back into the limbs, but in many cases it was too late. Several developed gangrene in fingers and toes, with the only alternative being amputation.

Captain Jacob Riley lay helpless, unable to move his legs. Terry worked with Carson, rubbing the captain's legs and flexing his knees while an occasional scream from the amputations echoed through the camp area.

Captain Riley tried to make light of his situation. "Looks like I'll be makin' more money than you, Kit. While you're sweatin' it out in the Army, I'll be sittin' on a street corner with no legs, sellin' pencils, thread and needles!"

Carson gritted his teeth as he worked with Riley's leg. "You might's well stop thinkin' like that, 'cause I ain't gonna let Jake Riley get the best o' me!"

Captain Riley miraculously recovered the use of his legs while the other men's amputations were cauterized and bandaged. Kit Carson decided to continue the foray through Canyon de Chelly with the survivors of Riley's company riding on some of the pack mules that had lesser loads, or sitting behind other soldiers on their horses.

When the company started out again, the going was arduous with the horses struggling through deep snow. The towering canyon walls held in cold shadows and each man pulled his greatcoat tighter.

At one point they heard distant shouts and looked up to see Indians moving from cave to cave like tiny blackbirds on the sheer cliffs. Their calls were a mixture of Indian and Spanish, taunting the soldiers below; however, the distance was so great, neither the Indians nor the white men could use a weapon against the other.

Kit Carson raised his steely eyes to the Indians. "We might not be able to catch 'em," he said, "but at least they know we're determined and it's no use fer 'em to keep runnin'."

The soldiers came to another wide area on the canyon floor where the Navajos grew patches of corn and wheat. A few hogans squatted nearby and the men rode over with guns ready. It was obvious that the Indians, like all the others before, had seen the white men's advance and quickly deserted the village.

One old woman, however, had been left behind, perhaps too feeble to make a fast getaway. She sat, swaddled in a blanket, beside a dying fire, and watched quietly as the soldiers rode up.

"We'll have to take her prisoner," Kit Carson said. "Somebody help her onto one o' the pack mules."

Terry and another man took the frail woman by the arms and helped her onto a mule. Terry looked at her wrinkled leathery face with its tired black eyes and wondered if she understood what was happening. He rode back to the front with Kit Carson and the group moved on slowly, their horses sinking into the deep drifts of snow.

They traveled all day with only an occasional sight of Indians high up on the canyon walls and Terry felt that the whole thing was useless since the only Indian they had taken was one old woman. They finally trotted out of the snow at the end of an adjoining canyon while the lowering sun was nearly lost in a hazy sky.

As the company began to make camp, Terry went in search of the captive woman to be sure she would be taken care of. The pack mule was there but the woman was nowhere in sight.

"Where is the old woman we took captive?" he asked the solder who had guided the mule.

The soldier gave him a sour look. "She couldn't stay on the mule. . .kept fallin' off. She was too much trouble, so we left her back in the canyon."

Terry stared in disbelief. "You left her?! She'll freeze or starve to death, you fool!"

The man sneered. "Come off it, soldier, she's just an old Indian!"

Terry rushed back to his horse and started to climb back into the saddle when Kit Carson walked over and grabbed the reins.

"Jest where do you think you're goin'?" Carson demanded.

"They left that old Indian woman back in the canyon," Terry replied. "Said she was too much trouble. . .I'm going to get her!"

Carson may have been shocked by the report but his face was as stony as ever. "Jest hold on. You cain't go back into that canyon. It'll be dark in a few minutes, an' if another blizzard hits, you're a goner!"

"But I've got to save that woman. . .she's starving and freezing to death!"

"Use yer head," Carson said and grabbed Terry's arm. "She's miles back and you'd be travelin' at night. Jest how do you know you could find her?!"

Terry seemed to fall apart inside and looked Kit Carson square into his hard, blue-gray eyes. "Are you telling me that it's all right to let that old woman die?"

"O' course it ain't!" Carson shouted back and the men close by turned with a start. "I'll peel the hide off those men fer leavin' her t'die, but I'm durned sure not gonna let one o' my men die, too!"

The two of them stood in angry silence, their eyes locked in silent combat. Finally Terry dropped his hands from the saddle and walked away.

Much later the men sat around a warming campfire in the black night, eating their supper of bacon, beans, hardtack and coffee, but Terry O'Neill could only pick at his food. He was still fuming with helpless anger, but even worse was his mounting resentment toward Kit Carson, the man he had once so greatly admired.

CHAPTER TWENTY-THREE

Willow-In-Storm pulled the blanket tighter around her shivering body and put another twig on the fire. The storm had passed, however deep snow still covered the entire valley and a cold wind moaned through the canyon's towering walls. The cattle had frozen or starved to death while everyone wondered if they would find enough roots or berries to sustain them another day. Chindi, the god of death, seemed to be waiting in each small hogan.

Standing Bear entered the stick-and-mud house and squatted down beside his niece. He rubbed his long cold fingers over the fire, trying to catch some warmth.

"Did you find the headman Manuelito?" Willow-In-Storm asked.

"Yes," Standing Bear replied. "He and his people were camped at the canyon mouth."

"And what was his decision?"

"Manuelito still refuses to surrender to the white men. He prefers to die in Dinetah."

Willow-In-Storm looked into the sad little fire. "Then that will be our fate also. . .to die in Dinetah?"

Standing Bear put his face down over his knees. "I cannot bear to hear the children crying from cold and hunger. . .to see our women turning into wrinkled corpses. Perhaps the gods will forgive us if we leave this sacred land. It seems to be the only way to keep the Diné from becoming extinct."

Willow-In-Storm shuddered, but not from the cold. "If we surrender, they will kill us anyway, like they murdered the others at the fort."

Her uncle raised his face. "Manuelito tells me that the ones who have surrendered are taken to another place to live. . .far to the west, away from Dinetah."

"And then murdered there?"

"He does not know. But the white men have burned the Diné's crops, killed our cattle and kept us from obtaining food. We must take the chance of surrender. It is either that, or starve and freeze to death here in Dinetah."

Chapter Twenty-Four

General Carleton raged at Bosque Redondo's sorry state of affairs and Governor Connelly was not happy.

"Fort Sumner still doesn't have proper facilities for the men," Connelly fretted, "and I hear the Indians are too drunk on their corn liquor to work on the buildings."

"Or till their fields," Carleton added. "If Sumner's commanding officer can't control the situation, I'll put someone there who can. Major Wallen is a hard-driving man. . .I'll assign him as the new commander and we'll see Bosque Redondo turn out to be what we expected!"

As soon as Major Wallen arrived at Fort Sumner, things changed dramatically. He not only stopped the Indians from manufacturing *tiswin*, but he pushed the fort's construction until there was a makeshift hospital and the enlisted men finally had a barracks.

"About time we got out of those damned tents!" Deacon Jones said as he plopped onto a bed for the first time in almost a year.

"I got a feelin' we're gonna pay for it!" Moony Calhoun told him. "That new commander's hard as nails. Wait and see, he's gonna have our butts draggin'!"

It was not far from the truth. Deacon and Moony found themselves driven hard, along with the other men, forcing the twenty-five hundred Apaches to clear four thousand acres of new land and enlarge the irrigation ditches. Soon, there was a surprisingly good yield of corn.

Even the superintendent of Indian Affairs Doctor Michael Steck was impressed when he visited the reservation. He had just returned from Washington, where his demeaning report of Bosque Redondo had fallen on deaf ears, and now he wondered if the trip had been made in vain.

Lorenzo Labadie, the Indian Agent living at the fort, gave Doctor Steck a tour of Bosque Redondo's fields where the tall corn stalks waved in a cold breeze.

"We have ten thousand pounds of corn in storage," Labadie said. "The quartermaster's even purchased unripened corn for the Army livestock. Now, the Indians have almost five hundred dollars credit posted at the sutler's store to buy whatever they need!"

Michael Steck nodded approvingly. "That's all very well for the Apaches you have, now," he replied, "but what are you going to do when twelve thousand Navajos start coming in?"

Labadie frowned. "I know this place can't hold them all. I've tried to talk General Carleton into keeping the Bosque as a reservation for the Apaches only, but he won't listen."

Steck gave a derisive laugh. "I've already tried that, but you can't talk sense into that man. He has this grandiose plan of bringing all the Indians together in one place to live happily ever after!" Then he looked grimly at his cohort. "If you and I work together, maybe we can side-track that plan."

CHAPTER TWENTY-FIVE

After their long cold trek through Canyon de Chelly, Colonel Kit Carson and his men trudged back to Fort Canby with discouragement. Only a few Navajos had been taken prisoner, mostly women and children. With almost no Indians to send to Bosque Redondo, Carson felt his campaign was a failure.

He was surprised, however to find Standing Bear and a large group of his people waiting at the fort for transportation to the Bosque Redondo reservation.

The old Indian not only spoke the white man's tongue, but was one of the wisest and most literate of all the Navajo headmen Kit Carson had known during his exploration of New Mexico and Colorado.

Carson could hardly believe his eyes. He raised his hand in a friendly greeting and rode up to the old Indian.

"Our people come in peace," Standing Bear said and also raised a friendly hand. "We have seen your great armies enter our land and hunt us down. You have burned our homes, destroyed our crops and cut down the peach trees that took many years to bear fruit. We have been deprived of raising food on the land that our ancestors gave us. We are tired of starving and wish no more killing."

"We don't want t'kill yer people," Carson told him. "We only want you t'live in peace at Bosque Redondo where the Army'll take care of you."

"I have talked with other headmen and told them that I trust whatever you say," Standing Bear said. "Many of them agree with me and are also bringing their people to join us."

Kit Carson was elated. "Does that include the great ones. . .Manuelito and Barboncito?"

"Barboncito, maybe, but not Manuelito. He swears to never leave the Dinetah."

Terry O'Neill sat on his horse, listening to the conversation. In the group of Indians behind Standing Bear, one young girl stood a little ahead of the others. She wore a long buckskin dress and beaded moccasins, her shiny black hair was tied back into a bun and her ebony eyes stared without a blink at the meeting between Carson and the old Indian. Terry thought that if the serious expression were taken from her smooth, light-bronze face she would be the prettiest Indian girl he had seen yet.

"We'll wait fer the others to arrive," Carson told the Indian. "Then I'll make arrangements so yer people can start fer Bosque Redondo as soon as possible."

It was a cold afternoon and the night would be near freezing. The soldiers gathered enough wood for the Indians to build small warming fires and, as darkness approached, Terry and a few others handed out the Navajos' food rations.

Terry spotted Standing Bear sitting on the ground next to a small fire while the Indian girl Terry had seen earlier in the day placed a blanket around the old man's shoulders. Terry carried the food over to them.

"Here is bread, and this is meat from deer the men killed this morning," Terry said. "And you can boil coffee with these ground beans."

Standing Bear only glanced at Terry without a reply and the girl's face was expressionless as she took the food.

"*Ahehee*," she said flatly. "Thank you. My father's brother is cold and the hot coffee will warm him."

Terry was held by her simple beauty and watched as she got on her knees to pour water into a pot for the coffee.

"I had an idea you two were related," Terry said. "My name is Terry O'Neill. . .what do they call you?"

She glanced at him in irritation and he thought she was going to ignore him, but the answer came while her back was turned. "They call me Willow-In-Storm."

Terry thought about it. "Willow-In-Storm. . .how did you come by that name?"

There was a long silence and it was obvious she wouldn't reply. Finally, her uncle spoke.

"She was a stubborn child," he said, still gazing into the fire. "Like the willow tree in a strong wind, its branches may bend, but they do not break."

"Well, anyway," Terry said, "I'm glad the Indians have agreed to come in peace. . .I sure don't want to see any more killing."

Willow-In-Storm looked up angrily. "We had no choice!" she spat at him. "What would you do if you had to choose between starvation and surrender?"

Terry felt as if he'd been slapped in the face. "I'm sorry," he said lamely.

"I guess I just don't understand the situation."

Her eyes were fierce with anger. "Even if you lived longer than my father's brother and your hair was white and your teeth falling out, you would never understand!"

The old Indian put a wrinkled hand on his niece's arm. "That will do," he told her and looked up at Terry. "You call us Navajos, but we are the Diné. When the Diné were first created, four mountains and four rivers were pointed out to us, inside of which we should live. This was to be our country, called the Dinetah, and was given to us by the Holy People from the spirit world. Our forefathers told us we were never to move east of the Rio Grande or west of the San Juan rivers. Dinetah is sacred land and the Diné would rather die than leave it. But now, the white man comes to take away our food and water. We cannot watch our children starve, our women shrivel up and produce no more babies. The Diné will surrender to the white eyes, but it is not because we love the *Bilagáana*."

"*Bilagáana?*" Terry asked in puzzlement.

"That is our word for the white men." Standing Bear turned his eyes back to the campfire. "If you can understand what I have told you, then it is good."

Terry swallowed hard. "I'm trying," he said quietly. "I really am." Then he nodded a polite goodbye and walked back to the fort.

More Navajos came in reluctantly until there was finally a large group camped outside the gates of Fort Canby. Kit Carson was happy to receive word that over a thousand more had surrendered at Fort Wingate and were waiting to be sent to Bosque Redondo. He hoped that with the Navajos at last starting to go to the Bosque Redondo, General Carleton would be pleased. Carson dictated a letter to the general.

"I'm sure you'll be glad t'know that I have about a hundred and sixty-five Navajos here at Canby that'll start movin' out soon and they'll pick up a good twelve hundred more at Fort Wingate. It's been hard work, especially in the winter cold, and more Navajos will be surrenderin' in the next few months. Since I feel my orders have been carried out, I humbly ask for leave to see my family in Taos for Christmas."

General Carleton answered promptly with his usual callous words:

"I cannot allow you to interrupt the campaign while it is just getting started. My orders are for you to go again to Canyon de Chelly and make a more thorough sweep of the Navajo stronghold. I especially want you to capture the most important one, Manuelito."

Another trek through Canyon de Chelly, especially in the middle of

December, was like a sentence of death and Terry wanted no part of it. He wished he could do the same as Kit Carson when things became discouraging, and that was to simply resign.

"With your permission, I'd like to be one of the escorts with the next group going to Bosque Redondo," he told Carson. "You'll be tied up at Canyon de Chelly for several months and won't need me."

Kit Carson slumped in his chair and Terry couldn't help feeling sorry for him. The colonel was now fifty-four years old and had done enough campaigning against the Indians to keep a hundred men busy. He raised his tired face and there was a rare twinkle in the steel-blue eyes.

"Cain't say as I blame you," he said. "I think I'd rather be walkin' to the Bosque myself, instead o' goin' back to that durned canyon in the dead o' winter. You go ahead. Reckon I'll be goin' to Fort Sumner soon, anyway, so we'll see each other then." He gave Terry a little grin. "If it'll make ye feel any better, I'll see to it you're a sergeant by the time you get there."

CHAPTER TWENTY-SIX

Terry pulled up his coat collar as he sat on a horse watching the Indians prepare for departure. They all knew the great distance to be covered and the merciless journey was being referred to as "The Long Walk."

As usual, the wagons had room for only the old and sick while the others were on foot. Terry's heart ached for them, knowing that three hundred miles of freezing weather lay ahead. Standing Bear clutched a blanket around his tall thin body and stood proudly erect at the head of the line. Willow-In-Storm, also wrapped in a blanket, was at his side and her dark eyes glinted with grim resignation.

As the group started out, Terry rode past the two Indians on his way to the rear of the party. He wanted to stop and tell the young girl how sorry he was about all this, but merely nodded with a tiny smile. Willow-In-Storm's hard expression never changed and she stared ahead as the ragged throng of humanity began moving slowly out of Fort Canby.

Those who could walk stretched across the plains in double file while the old wrinkled squaws sat on top of the supply wagons. Next to them lay the ones weak with dysentery and stomach cramps from the strange white man's food at Fort Canby.

John Thompson, now a Major, was in command of the sixty soldiers riding escort, which included Terry, Nicholas Hodt and four other captains.

While Terry and Captain Hodt rode guard at the rear, making sure none of the Indians decided to turn back, Hodt noticed Terry's expression of futile pity.

"At least the first leg of the trip to Fort Wingate is a short one," Hodt said.

"We'll have to cross the Puerco River first," Terry replied. "You think we'll have any problems?"

"It's a small river. We'll have our real problem at the Rio Grande, and maybe the Pecos."

The sun was low and a cold wind blew across the group when they arrived at the Puerco River. As Captain Hodt had predicted, it was narrow, however the water was frigid and waist deep.

The commander John Thompson was kind enough to let most of the women and children ride behind on horseback as they waded across the rushing stream, but the others were forced to slosh across to the opposite bank, climbing out with wet, numbed legs and feet.

Some of the Indians were barely able to walk with their frozen limbs when the party arrived at Fort Wingate late in the day. The Navajos who had already arrived at the fort greeted their suffering kinsmen and helped them put up temporary shelters with warming fires. Terry was not surprised to see that the food given out was the same inadequate rations the Indians had received beforehand.

The post commander rode out to make an inspection of the wretched encampment and decided things were going well.

"General Carleton's orders are to let them rest here for three days before going on to Fort Sumner," he told the escort officers.

"Well, that's mighty kind of the general," Nicholas Hodt said in a low voice to Terry. "They can rest up before another three hundred miles!"

The morning was dark and biting with frost when the Indians were forced to start out again. Terry hoped, as they moved down to the flatlands, that the cold would ease up but it followed them like a mountain lion stalking its prey. He watched with a growing compassion as the older Indians struggled to keep on their feet.

Captain Hodt glanced at Terry's anguished face.

"I know how you feel," Hodt said, "but try not to think about it. If you let all this get to you, you'll go crazy!" He took the flask from his coat and held it out. "Here, maybe this will help."

Terry looked at it with scorn. "No, thanks."

The captain took a swig and returned the flask to his pocket as they continued riding.

A moment later Terry saw one old woman fall to her knees and he reined his horse to a stop. "I'm going to let that woman ride behind me!" He started to turn the horse around but Hodt grabbed the reins.

"Hold on," the captain said. "Not only is it against orders, but you'd just stir up trouble."

Terry gave him an angry look. "How could it cause trouble?"

"If you showed a preference to one of those Indians, they'd all start demanding a ride. We have a long way to go and you know a horse won't last long with two riders on his back!"

Terry sat for a moment and watched the woman rubbing her bare feet. "But her moccasins are gone. . .the least I can do is help!"

Captain Hodt watched as Terry rode over to the woman. While the group moved slowly onward, Terry dismounted and took one of his blankets from the saddle. He had to use his teeth to rip off several pieces of the blanket, which he wrapped around the woman's feet. When he lifted her up by the arms, she began hobbling forward and a young Indian girl ran over to help the woman catch up with the party.

Terry got back onto his horse with the small remainder of the blanket and rejoined Captain Hodt who gave him a rewarding smile.

"You're going to sleep cold tonight," Hodt said.

Terry shrugged in irritation. "Not as cold as a lot of these Indians!"

The night was indeed a freezing one and the small fires gave little comfort after they had made camp. It was difficult to spot Willow-In-Storm and her uncle in the crowd and Terry wondered how they were making out. He was especially concerned for the babies, but the mothers sacrificed their blankets to keep the little ones as warm as possible.

They continued pushing their aching bodies onward across the cold hard sand and at midday the sky darkened to an ominous purple.

Terry looked up with a groan. "Not a blue norther—that's all these people need!"

Soon the temperature plunged and an icy wind swept across the plains. When snowflakes began swirling around them, Major Thompson decided to make camp until the storm had passed. Because of the wind, it was impossible to keep a fire going. The soldiers had small dog tents for protection but the Indians had only their blankets and the area was soon covered with shivering bodies huddled together for warmth.

Terry trembled with cold in his greatcoat and knew that the Navajos were suffering even more. It was impossible to think that any of them would survive the bone-chilling night; he felt like it was the end of the world as the wind howled over him.

By morning the storm had gone its way and Terry was thankful to see a warm sun rising in the clear sky. When the group aroused themselves from the layer of snow to build fires, Terry walked among the pitiful huddled forms, looking for Willow-In-Storm. Some of the Indians sat with tearful faces beside the stiff, frozen bodies of their loved ones who had closed their eyes during the night and never awakened.

Finally, Terry spotted Standing Bear who was on his haunches before a tiny fire, grasping a blanket tightly around his thin body. But the Indian was alone and Terry's heart sank. He hurried over to the old man.

"Your niece, Willow-In-Storm," Terry said, "I don't see her. . .is she all right?"

Standing Bear raised his tired eyes for only a glance to see who was addressing him and then looked back into the small fire.

"She is more fortunate than some of the others," the old man replied. "She has gone for water to make coffee."

"I'm glad to know you both survived the night," Terry said. With nothing more worthy to add, he returned to the soldiers' campfire.

The ground was too hard to dig graves, therefore the bodies of the dead Indians were left to thaw and be torn apart by coyotes and vultures. Then the group trudged painfully onward to face their next test of will—the Rio Grande.

When they eventually came to the river it was swollen with rushing cold water from melted snow by the storm that had swept down from the north. Major Thompson ordered the women and children to ride behind the soldiers or cling to the wagons as the party began its dangerous crossing. The less fortunate formed human chains, clinging tightly to each other's hands as they waded into the freezing water that swirled almost to their chins.

Terry guided his horse down into the river, hoping he would find Willow-In-Storm and her uncle safe on the other bank. Suddenly he heard screams over the roaring water and turned to see that the chain was broken. Two women had been swept away and were fighting to keep their heads above water as the angry river carried them downstream.

Terry urged the horse around quickly to reach the women. He jumped from his saddle into the icy torrent and clutched one of them by the arm, but she slipped away to disappear beneath the surface. He struggled in the chest-deep water, searching in despair, but there was no sign of the women. With a choke of defeat he climbed back onto the horse and made his way out of the freezing river.

As he rode up the bank he saw through watery eyes that Willow-In-Storm had made it across and was watching with the others. His soaked body was numb from cold when he stopped the horse in front of the girl, happy to see that she was all right. Willow-In-Storm looked at him and, for a moment, he thought he spotted a hint of gratitude in her dark eyes—but she turned and went to join her uncle.

Before going on, Major Thompson ordered fires to be built so the freezing survivors of the crossing could dry out. By midday they began moving eastward again. Terry's clothing was still damp and he raised his face to the noon sun, thankful for its warmth.

The dried plains soon turned to a hot skillet of sand beneath the Indians' cut and bruised feet. Their moccasins had worn out and a trail of blood dotted the ground behind them. Those with lacerated feet and broken toenails who could no longer walk were crowded onto the wagons, but the mules could pull only so much while the hardier ones struggled behind, trying to keep up the pace.

Terry and Captain Hodt, riding at the rear, eventually came upon two women who had fallen out of line while the group of suffering humanity kept moving. Terry was surprised to see that the younger Indian was Willow-In-Storm and she crouched on the ground, giving solace to the older woman who was obviously pregnant.

"Wait a minute," Terry said to Nicholas Hodt. "We've got to help them!"

They stopped and got down from their horses.

"Willow-In-Storm," Terry said, "can I help?"

The girl looked up at him with controlled emotions. "This woman is late with her child. She cannot walk any more."

Major Thompson had seen his two men stop and rode over to find the reason.

"What's the trouble here?" the major asked.

"The woman's pregnant," Terry replied. "We'll have to put her on one of the wagons."

"The wagons can't take any more," Thompson said.

"Then maybe we can wait till she's all right," Terry countered, knowing it was wrong to argue with a superior.

"You know we can't hold up the party, Sergeant," Thompson replied with irritation. "Now, get this other girl back in line." He turned to Nicholas Hodt. "We'll be making camp in a few hours, Captain." He glanced down at the suffering woman. "If that one can't keep up, I want you to take care of the situation!" He moved his horse around and rode back to the front.

Terry looked with confusion at Nicholas Hodt and the captain gritted his teeth in a decision.

"Do what the major says," Hodt said, "and take this young girl back to join the others. I'll tend to the woman."

Terry felt helpless and looked down at Willow-In-Storm. "Come on, now," he told her gently, "we'll have to do what the major ordered."

"But if we leave her, she will die!"

"It'll be all right." He helped Willow-In-Storm to her feet.

With a worried backward glance, the girl walked away to join the others and Terry got back into his saddle. He gave Nicholas Hodt another concerned look. "Need any help?" he asked.

The captain's face was stony. "I'll take care of it."

Terry rejoined the group and rode slowly, making sure Willow-In-Storm had gone back to join her uncle at the head of the line. A moment later Terry heard a gunshot and he suddenly wanted to vomit.

Darkness fell quickly. After they made camp, the soldiers sat around the campfire, eating, but Nicholas Hodt was not present. Terry ate very little, for he had no appetite. He put down his tin plate and saw the captain's shadowy figure leaning against a saddle where the horses were tethered.

Terry took a deep breath and walked over to Hodt in the secluded darkness. The captain was taking swigs from a whiskey bottle, which surprised Terry. Even though drinking was against regulations, Captain Hodt had still nursed his flask; but the bottle, now, was a flagrant disobedience.

"Where did you get the bottle?" Terry asked quietly.

Hodt didn't look up. "A sergeant sneaked it to me. . .for a good price, I might add."

Terry breathed in the cold night air and shivered. "That's not going to help. Nothing will. After what happened today, I hated you for it. But I remembered what you told me once, back at Fort Stanton—we're all in this and there's nothing we can do about it. If you want to call it humane, it was probably the only thing you could've done." He sighed, remembering his favorite horse Rusty Rose at the New York riding stables; when the mare broke her leg it had to be destroyed. "Like shooting a horse when it can't walk any more, I guess."

The dim starlight caught a glint of anger in the captain's eyes. "You're right, Sergeant. But right now, I am ashamed to be a representative of this damned United States Army!"

Terry knew he couldn't leave Captain Hodt to drink the rest of the night—he would be in no condition to walk the next morning and a court-martial would surely result.

"We have to get some sleep for an early start tomorrow," Terry said. "Why don't you give me that bottle and get into your blanket. I'll hide the whiskey for you in my saddlebags."

Hodt thought for a moment and then shrugged. He took one last swig, stamped the cork into the bottle and handed it to Terry. "Go ahead and get your rest. I'll sleep it off here."

Terry hesitated, then put the bottle in his coat and walked back to the warmth of the dying campfire. He slipped the bottle, unseen, into his saddlebags and rolled up in the blanket, but the day's horrible incident refused to let him sleep.

While the gentle snoring from the other men filled the night air, Terry lay staring at the sky that seemed to be filled with twinkling diamonds. He tried to rid his mind of the terrible events in the last few days and turned over with a groan. He was almost asleep when a muffled gunshot cut the night's silence and the tethered horses whinnied in fright. The men rose up, quickly awakened.

"Somebody's stealin' our horses!" one of them said.

Terry sat up and wrapped the blanket around his shoulders as two of the men ran to the horse area. They found all the animals safely tethered, but Terry's heart froze when he heard another man shout.

"My God, it's Captain Hodt. . .he's blown his brains out!"

CHAPTER TWENTY-SEVEN

Perhaps the only thing that kept the Indians going was the white man's promise of food and new hogans awaiting them at the end of their torturous journey. They eventually reached the Pecos River and crossed it without incident, with Fort Sumner and Bosque Redondo waiting on the opposite bank. However, when the exhausted group straggled in, wet and hungry, they found only more despair.

The Indians were herded like cattle into a line to be counted, then were forced to dig large holes in the ground for shelter. Tree limbs were laid overhead, but it did little to keep out the icy winds. The few thin blankets handed out were poor protection while the rations were almost inedible and not enough to feed every hungry mouth.

Terry felt guilty as he went to the comfortable barracks, but was cheered somewhat by a welcome from Deacon Jones and Moony Calhoun. They noticed the stripes on Terry's sleeve right away.

"Well, look at Sergeant O'Neill, here!" Deacon said. He turned to Moony. "We're gonna have to watch our step with a NCO in the barracks, now!"

"We been keepin' the place warm fer you!" Moony said to Terry. "Where's ol' Grizzly and the others?"

"They're all dead," Terry replied. "Killed by an avalanche at Canyon de Chelly."

There was a moment of surprise.

"I guess none of us can live forever," Moony said, shaking his head.

Terry shot him an angry look. "Did you have to say that?!"

Deacon cut the tension. "Well, Sergeant O'Neill, after a couple o' days here at Fort Sumner, you're gonna wish you'd never left Fort Stanton . . .wait'll you take a look around this hell hole!"

Terry saw the truth in Deacon's words the next day when the Indians were assembled to begin work. Terry went with ten other soldiers to the Apache camp, south on the reservation, and saw the pitiful living conditions. The hovels were obviously no protection from the fierce weather of northern New Mexico and the air was laden with the foul smell of inadequate sanitary facilities.

Terry and the other soldiers herded the Apaches to an area where a large irrigation ditch was being dug to bring water from the Pecos River to their fields. Proper tools were scarce and many of the Indians clawed out the hard earth with their bare hands.

It was another sad Christmas for Terry, made even more lonely with the absence of his good friend, Ben Adams. With food being such a scarce commodity, there was no festive dinner like the ones Terry remembered when he visited his parents at Monmouth, or the sumptuous holiday meals at the Godfreys' comfortable New York home. Terry spent his time writing letters and counted the days when he would be able to hold Susan in his arms once more.

Agent Labadie finally received more farming implements by the time warm weather moved in and the Navajos were put to work clearing land for their crops.

Terry was one of the groups that began supervising the Indians as they went to the fields early each morning and his heart quickened when he saw a familiar face among the Navajos.

"Willow-In-Storm!" he called and ran over to the young girl who was in a group carrying picks and hoes. "Do you remember me. . .Terry O'Neill?"

She stopped and turned to him. Her young face was tired and still held the look of contempt he had seen when they first met.

"What do you wish of me, Teri-O-Neel?" she asked.

It warmed his heart the way she spoke his name as one word—much like her own was pronounced.

"I'm just glad to see you again," he replied, "and that you made the journey all right." He looked around at the Indians. "I don't see your uncle, Standing Bear. . .is he all right?"

"The tribal leaders are not made to work," she told him, "but he is like the others. . .hungry and longing for our Dinetah."

She turned and started to join the others.

"Wait!" Terry said and caught up with her. "Maybe I can help. . .I'll bring you more food."

She kept walking. "We cannot accept·your gifts," "If we did so, the others would hate us."

"All right, then," Terry said in frustration, "Can't we just be friends?"

She stopped only to give him a hard look. "You still do not understand," she said and continued to the fields with the other Indians.

Terry stood looking helpless. He felt a small growing anger but didn't know if it was directed at himself or at Willow-In-Storm.

The Navajos, having seen the Apaches' already sprouting fields, worked diligently to emulate their enemy and, when early summer arrived, all the crops were green with the Indians in both camps feeling a small pride in their accomplishments.

However, there was animosity between the two and the Apaches sneaked into Navajo fields to destroy the enemy's crops. Navajos retaliated by entering the Apache cornfields and began cutting down the stalks until fighting broke out.

Rakes, hoes and sticks were used as weapons and the soldiers ran to stop the Indians from killing each other. Terry saw Willow-In-Storm scratching in fury at a Mescalero woman as another Apache struck Willow-In-Storm's leg with a sharp hoe. The girl shrieked in pain and fell to the ground, clutching at her ankle. Terry ran over and dropped to her side as the battling was subdued by the other soldiers.

"That's a bad cut," Terry said. "Let me wrap my kerchief around it."

Willow-In-Storm's anger had not disappeared and she lay panting while Terry tried to bandage the wound, but the blood still came in a small crimson pool among the dry brown leaves.

"I'd better get you to the hospital," he said and helped her to her feet, but she couldn't stand.

The girl remained silent as Terry picked her up in his arms and started out for the hospital.

The makeshift adobe building was some distance away and he was puffing when they went inside. Post Surgeon George Gwyther saw them and quickly made space on a large table he used for operating.

"Here's your first patient for the day," Terry said to the doctor as he gently placed Willow-In-Storm onto the table, "but there'll be more coming behind me."

"Well, that's what I'm here for," the doctor said and examined Willow-In-Storm's nasty wound.

After Gwyther had bandaged the girl's leg, five more Indians came in with head and arm wounds and he went to work on them while Terry placed Willow-In-Storm onto a nearby cot.

"I know you're in a lot of pain," he said. "You're a brave girl not to even make a face."

She lay in silence, staring at him.

"Well," he said awkwardly, "guess that's all I can do. You'll be taken good care of here."

He started to leave and she put out her hand, lightly touching his sleeve. "Teri-O-Neel," she said. "I must thank you for helping me."

He looked at her in surprise and the tiny anger in his heart vanished when he saw a faint gentleness in the shiny black eyes.

CHAPTER TWENTY-EIGHT

"Didn't I tell you," General Carleton chortled to Governor Connelly, "Kit Carson was the right man for this job! His latest swing through Canyon de Chelly has brought the surrender of hundreds of Navajos! Now, there are thousands walking to Bosque Redondo!"

The governor shifted uncomfortably in his chair. "Yes, but there are nasty rumors of some of them being shot or left to die when they get sick and fall out of line. I certainly don't want these kinds of reports getting back to Washington."

"It won't mean a thing after they receive my message," Carleton said. "I'm telling them the successful campaign against the Navajos is a crowning act by the famous scout and Indian fighter, Kit Carson. His name alone will make them forget any rumors of cruelty."

Fort Sumner's commander Major Wallen looked at the matter with a different eye and shook his head in frustration as crowds of Navajos swelled Bosque Redondo's population.

"If that damned general in Santa Fe wants to flood me with Indians," Wallen said to his adjutant, "where is the food he's promised?! The ones we have now are starving and too weak to build even the shoddiest houses!"

"They're not the only ones hungry," the adjutant replied. "Since Carleton's cut rations at every fort in New Mexico, we're all feeling it!"

Terry found it difficult to enjoy his own reduced meals, knowing of the hunger pains gouging each Indian stomach. When he went to the mess hall, he took an extra tin plate and scraped most of his meat and bread into the plate. Moony Calhoun, sitting beside him, watched with curiosity.

"You takin' that back to the barracks with you?" he asked.

"No," Terry said. "I'm taking it to some Indians who need it more than I do."

Moony pushed his plate over to Terry. "I know what you mean—it hurts me, too, seein' 'em go hungry like that. Here, take some of mine."

Terry covered the plate of food and took it to Standing Bear's hogan.

"I know you're hungry," he told the Indian. "The others haven't seen me come here, so you can take this food."

Standing Bear glanced down at the plate. It was a great temptation, but he looked back at Terry. "It would be like stones in our mouths, knowing that the others did not have any."

Willow-In-Storm, who had been listening, appeared at her uncle's side. She turned her sad dark eyes onto Terry.

"Your heart is big, Teri-O-Neel. But my father's brother speaks the truth. . .we could never swallow your food if the others could not swallow it also."

Terry was torn by guilt and frustration. On his way back to the fort, he looked down at the food in his hand. He was hungry but knew if he ate it, the bread and meat would be like stones in his mouth, too. He set the plate down at the door of a scrubby hogan and went on to the barracks.

The next day Terry watched from the enlisted men's quarters as the Indians lined up for their rations. Only the young had come for their food since the older ones were no doubt too weak to stand in line. Terry shook his head sadly and decided to go check on his horse, hoping to clear his mind of the depressing sight.

He found Willow-In-Storm standing beside the Army corral, holding a clay bowl partially filled with dirty kernels of corn. Two Navajo children were inside the corral, down on their haunches, poking sticks among the manure from the horses and Terry wondered if they were playing some kind of strange Indian game.

"What are the children doing?" Terry asked.

Willow-In-Storm lowered her eyes. "They find corn that the horses have not digested."

Terry looked at the bowl of corn in her hands. "You mean you're eating this?"

She looked up. "After it is washed, we boil it or fry it. It is food."

The look of despair in her eyes stabbed at Terry's heart and he wanted to take her in his arms. He clenched his fists instead. "I'm told that a wagon train of food supplies will arrive in two days. . .I'll see to it that you and your uncle get your share right away."

But the Comanches had stepped up their raids in the Panhandle and only a few wagon trains from the east got through. Major Wallen was sitting at his desk, head in hands when his adjutant approached hesitantly.

"Sir," the soldier began, "I have to report that Captain McCleave has just come in from Fort Wingate with more prisoners."

The major raised his blood-shot eyes. "I'm afraid to ask," he mumbled, "but how many this time?"

The adjutant gulped. "Over twenty-two hundred, sir!"

While the Indians were being counted, Captain William McCleave reported to the post commander.

"I was assigned nearly twenty-five hundred," McCleave said, "but over a hundred died at Fort Wingate before we even got started. Then, with blizzards, short rations and the river crossings, we lost another hundred and ninety-seven men women and children."

"I won't ask how many you had to shoot when they couldn't keep up the pace!" Major Wallen replied sourly. "Now, let's go see what you've brought me."

The post commander went outside with Captain McCleave to look at the pitiful crowd of Navajos sitting, exhausted, on the ground while they were counted.

"You see that determined one over there?" McCleave said, pointing to a particular Indian. "He's Barboncito. . .one of the biggest Navajo headmen!"

"That'll make General Carleton happy," Major Wallen said, "but the one he really wants is old Manuelito." Wallen laughed. "It's like a thorn in the general's side, the way Manuelito keeps hiding and refusing to surrender!"

Chief Barboncito sat on the hard ground, taking in the bleak surroundings, and his black eyes flashed with hatred. Most of his cattle had died or were stolen while the white men had deprived his people of food and shelter. To keep them from dying of starvation and cold, Barboncito had no choice but to lead his people into surrender and take the grueling Long Walk to Bosque Redondo. But he would not remain in this inhospitable place; there were no fences, only guards, and it would be easy to escape during the night. He would bide his time.

When Terry, Deacon and Moony walked out of their barracks the next morning, they saw the banks of the Pecos River turning into a pitiful sight; brush-and-mud huts of starving, half-naked Navajos stretched for fifteen miles. Terry's heart sank, thinking of Willow-In-Storm and her uncle trying to exist in such misery.

"That general in Santa Fe must be crazy!" Deacon said.

Moony gave a snort. "He oughta come down here and see jest what he's created!"

In Santa Fe, General Carleton paced the floor with mounting concern as he clutched the latest report from Major Wallen. But the general's concern was not with the starving Indians.

"It's that Indian Agent Lorenzo Labadie!" the general complained to Governor Connelly. "Major Wallen tells me the Navajos are angry after being told by Labadie that they're trespassing on an Apache reservation and will be sent to another location!"

"You're going to have to get firm with those government people," Connelly said. "See if you can get them out of our hair!"

After the governor left, General Carleton summoned his adjutant and dictated a reply to Major Wallen at Fort Sumner:

"Advise Agent Lorenzo Labadie that if he causes further trouble, he will be expelled from Bosque Redondo. This order also applies to all Indian Department personnel—specifically Doctor Michael Steck. Remind these two that even though the War Department has not yet been given complete control of the Indians, I am still running the Bosque Redondo reservation."

The beleaguered commander at Fort Sumner was further aggravated to awake one morning and learn that the headman Barboncito, with nearly five hundred Navajos, had silently departed Bosque Redondo during the night.

"Send all available cavalry after them!" Major Wallen ordered.

"But we can take only forty-four men," Captain McCleave replied.

"Go ahead, anyway," the aggrieved commander said. "I'll notify General Carleton and tell him that's all we can do."

The air around Santa Fe grew hotter with General Carleton's fury after learning that so many Navajos had escaped.

"Have all the soldiers from Fort Craig go after them," he spouted. "And ask all citizens of southern New Mexico to join in the hunt. We must either kill the renegades or bring them back to Bosque Redondo!"

Soon hundreds of troops were scouring the plains and mountains, but Barboncito was too clever. He and his people safely hid out in Apache country and eluded capture.

The next meeting between General Carleton and Governor Connelly was not as cordial as their earlier ones.

"Your dream of a 'Fair Carletonia' is becoming an ugly monster, growing out of control!" the governor said. "If something isn't done soon, I can see both our careers going up in smoke!"

"Food is the biggest problem," Carleton said. "The Indians can't be happy if they're hungry."

"Well, we've been pushing Washington as hard as we can, and more shipments will be coming next week, thank goodness! But the Indians are still going to be discontent."

Carleton thought a moment and then grinned slyly. "By Jove, why haven't I thought of this before!"

"What miracle have you come up with, now?" Connelly asked bitterly.

"I need someone at Bosque Redondo who can keep the Indians satisfied with their new mode of life, and Kit Carson's the one to do it! I'll send him there immediately, and give him the title of Military Superintendent of Indians."

Carson had fortunately not seen the earlier disastrous conditions at the reservation and by the time he arrived, the Apache and Navajo crops were ripening while food rations had improved.

Terry O'Neill met Kit Carson with mixed feelings; he wondered if Kit Carson realized the horrors that had taken place on the Long Walks.

"I've held council with several of the tribal leaders here at the Bosque," Carson said to Terry, "and if you will, I'd like to send a report to General Carleton."

Terry readied himself with pencil and paper and began to write as Carson dictated:

"The Indians at Bosque Redondo seem content and are workin' hard t'make a success of their new life. The exodus of this whole people from the land of their fathers is a touchin' sight. They've fought us gallantly and defended their mountains and canyons with heroism. They've sacrificed their beautiful country and traditions to the progress of our race. As brave men, they are entitled to our admiration and respect and we should not dole out a miser's pittance in return."

Carson paused for a long moment and Terry looked up from the paper. "That's an eloquent statement," he said. "Is that all?"

"No," Carson replied, "I have one more thing to say."

Terry started writing again while Carson continued.

"Now that both the Apaches and Navajos have surrendered and been delivered to Bosque Redondo as you ordered, I feel that my assignment has been accomplished. I've been separated from my family fer too long durin' these past two years and therefore I ask that you accept my resignation so that I can return to my duties as husband and father."

After Kit Carson signed the letter and it was sent it off by courier, Terry thought with amusement how the colonel's other requests to resign had been ignored. He wondered what kind of ruse Carleton would dream up this time to hold Carson under his thumb.

CHAPTER TWENTY-NINE

General Carleton chortled with delight as he read a reply from Secretary of War Edwin Stanton.

"Finally, some good news for a change!" he told Governor Connelly. "You'll remember my complaints to the Secretary of War about Labadie's failure to get a farm started by the Apaches and his constant interference at the Bosque? Well, just listen to Stanton's reply."

Carleton held the paper up and began to read:

"Indian agents should not be permitted to interfere or exercise any authority on this military reservation. As of this date, the military will have absolute control."

General Carleton dropped the paper on his desk. "Now," he said, rubbing his hands together, "I can get tough with Lorenzo Labadie!"

The general summoned his adjutant and, as Governor Connelly sat listening, Carleton dictated a prompt message to Agent Labadie at Fort Sumner; it had the effect of a slashing saber:

"The Bosque Redondo reservation is now under sole charge of the military. Therefore, your services upon the reservation are no longer required. You have ten days to prepare for your departure. If you have not left by that time, the military will escort you bodily from the reservation!"

After the adjutant had left to forward the message, General Carleton sat behind his desk with satisfaction.

"Well," he said, "I'm relieved of one trouble-maker, but Michael Steck is still fighting to get the Navajos returned to their own country and there's nothing I can do to keep that man quiet!"

"Don't let Micahael Steck upset you," Governor Connelly said. "You know, as well as I, that Washington hardly listens to us, anyway! You should be happy that the Navajos have been defeated."

"Not really. I won't rest until every last one of them is at Bosque Redondo. . .and the most important one is old Manuelito. I've even given orders to hunt him down, and shoot him without mercy if he won't surrender, but he's still hiding out there somewhere!"

"If Manuelito's so respected by all the Navajos," Connelly said, "maybe you could get one of the headmen at the Bosque to go talk with him. Use persuasion instead of force."

"But if I let one of them return to his land, he'd just stay there and not come back."

"Pick a man who'd have to leave his family at the Bosque. . .one who'd want to come back to his loved ones."

Carleton rubbed his chin in thought. "You may be right. I'll send a message to Major Wallen right away."

The gentle warmth of late summer spread over Fort Sumner's few completed buildings while activity on those still under construction eased to a lazy pace. The golden rays of a morning sun even helped to soften the wretched face of Bosque Redondo with its hovels of ragged, hungry Indians.

Major Wallen read General Carleton's message and summoned Standing Bear for a conference. Even though it was a warm day, the old Indian wrapped a handsome blanket around his shoulders and appeared in Wallen's office.

"The Navajo headman called Manuelito is still evading the Army and refuses to come to Bosque Redondo," Wallen told the Indian. "General Carleton knows that Manuelito will listen to you. The general has given orders to let you return to your country for a short time if you will talk with Manuelito and urge him to come back to Bosque Redondo with you."

Standing Bear warmed at the thought of going back to his own country, for seeing Dinetah again would bring the sun into his heart.

"Manuelito is a *rico*," Standing Bear said, "and I think the only way to change his mind is to take away his cattle and food. I will talk with him, but I cannot promise that he will agree to leave his land."

Major Wallen smiled with confidence. "Good! I'll have an officer and some of the soldiers go with you as an escort."

"That is not good," Standing Bear replied. "Manuelito hides from the white man. If I go with an officer and soldiers, Manuelito would never let me approach. It is better to take just one man. I know of only one soldier here whose heart is for the welfare of our people. If I trust that soldier, Manuelito will trust him, also."

"And who is this man?"

"His name is Sergeant Terry O'Neill."

Major Wallen had to concede, for he dreaded General Carleton's wrath if the meeting with Manuelito didn't go through.

"All right," Wallen replied, "but O'Neill is only a sergeant. . .he'll have to take an officer with him."

"An officer would represent the white man's total authority. Let only young Sergeant O'Neill go with me or it will be useless to find Manuelito."

Terry was both flattered and humbled by Standing Bear's choice for an escort. At Major Wallen's insistence, Terry was equipped with a pistol at his hip and rifle slung on the saddle, then he and Standing Bear left with ample provisions the following morning.

They rode for several days toward the west until they were at a point just southwest of Albuquerque when Standing Bear stopped his horse and gazed at the western sky. Terry realized that they were at the edge of Navajo country and he stopped his horse, also.

In the distance was Mount Taylor, a sacred mountain called *Tsoodzil* by the Navajos; it marked the southern boundary of their land of Dinetah. The majestic peak stood like a huge silent god on the plains of crowded sage and distant piñons while the sky glowed in the background with streaks of gold and yellow.

Standing Bear slowly climbed down from the horse and got to his knees on the warm desert sand. He lowered his forehead to the ground with outstretched arms and Terry could almost feel the old Indian thanking the Holy People for letting him come back to the land given to the Navajos by their ancestors so many centuries ago.

Terry sat in reverent silence until Standing Bear climbed back into the saddle. Two lines of moisture ran down the Navajo's bronze cheeks, sparkling in the morning sun, and Terry had to fight a blur that swelled in his own eyes.

They continued west until sundown and reached the village of Zuñi Pueblo. One of the older Indian men received them warmly, providing food and wood for a fire. The man told Standing Bear that Chief Manuelito was in the vicinity.

"Manuelito knows that you have returned to your land and waits to see you once more," the elderly man said.

"Where can I find him?" Standing Bear asked.

"Only you are to know where he is. If you ride ten miles to the southwest, there is a place called Deer Springs. Manuelito's camp is there." The Indian glanced suspiciously at Terry. "But he hides from the white soldiers and his camp is well guarded."

Early next morning Terry and Standing Bear rode to the southwest until they were stopped by a shout from one of the towering redstone cliffs. Terry squinted but couldn't see anyone among the rocks. Standing Bear's sharp eyes, however, caught the figure of one of his people; he answered in a loud voice and there was a fast reply.

After another call, Standing Bear turned to Terry.

"This is Manuelito's camp," the Indian said. "They don't want a white soldier to come with me, but I told them you are a good friend. It is safe for us to enter, now."

The camp was well hidden among cliffs studded with Indian braves holding rifles. Terry rode behind Standing Bear as they entered the area where a few sad makeshift hogans stood around a fire pit. Nearby was a crude corral holding a small group of haggard-looking sheep. Two Indian braves, carrying rifles, appeared and spoke to Standing Bear who translated the words for Terry.

"You will have to leave your weapons here," the old Indian said.

Terry took off his gun belt and hung it over the saddlehorn along with the rifle, then he and Standing Bear dismounted.

Another Indian emerged from one of the hogans to greet them. He wore only loose cotton trousers and knee-length deerskin boots. Around his neck were strands of white and red beads holding two sharp animal bones that rested on his bare chest. He was not a muscular man, but the arms and stomach were firm. His gray-black hair was short and straight while the face was gravely determined. The commanding look in his stern eyes gave no doubt that he was the great headman Manuelito.

The two Indians greeted each other with a warm embrace and Standing Bear introduced Terry. Manuelito sized him up with discerning black eyes and then showed the newcomers into his hogan.

As Terry's eyes adjusted quickly to the inside shadows, he saw that a Navajo woman sat among animal furs next to the far wall. It looked as though she were sewing skins together and she paused to look up at the strangers.

"This is my wife Juanita," Manuelito told them. "It is all right for us to talk here."

The woman said nothing and continued her work while the men sat cross-legged on skins spread over the ground.

"The Great White Chief has sent me to ask you to come back with us to the reservation," Standing Bear began. "I have brought Sergeant O'Neill with me, for he must take the words we speak back with him, so I will translate what we say."

Manuelito nodded in agreement.

"Your sheep look weak and hungry," Standing Bear continued, "and your horses are in no better condition."

Manuelito answered glumly. "If it were only the white men who chased us, it would not be so bad. We can hide from them. But we are attacked by the Utes, the Pueblos, the Hopi, Mexicans and Anglos. They steal our sheep and horses. What cattle we have left cannot find enough food. Even my people are living on wild roots, cactus and berries."

"There is only one hope for you and your people," Standing Bear said. "At the Bosque Redondo reservation, the white man will give you food and clothing. They will protect you from raids of your enemies."

"My people are afraid to go to a reservation. They remember how the people were gathered together by the white man at the fort years ago and were murdered there. They believe that is the reason for a reservation."

"That is not true," Standing Bear replied. "Have they killed me? Or the daughter of my brother who is still there?"

Manuelito shook his head. "But this is the Dinetah. . .our sacred ground given to us by the spirit world. The Holy People told us we were never to go beyond the rivers that encircle the Dinetah or disaster would befall us."

Standing Bear looked through the hogan doorway at the pitiful herd of sheep and sick horses. "With what you have here and your enemies slowly destroying you, is this not disaster also?"

The old Indian's eyes filled with a determined sadness. "I cannot go to the reservation. My God and my mother live here and I will not leave them, even if I must suffer all the consequences of war and famine."

Then Manuelito turned to look into Terry's eyes and spoke directly to him as Standing Bear translated the words.

"Tell your Great White Chief that I have never done any wrong to the Americans or Mexicans. I have never robbed or killed them. I have always lived on my own resources. Tell your Great Chief to come and try to take me whenever he pleases, but I would rather die here than to leave the Dinetah. If I am killed, innocent blood will be shed."

Seeing that it was useless to change Manuelito's mind, Terry and Standing Bear started their ride back to Fort Sumner under a cloud of gloom. Terry felt sorry for the proud Manuelito and could see no way out of the old Indian's dilemma.

"What do you think will become of Manuelito?" Terry asked Standing Bear who rode somberly alongside.

"Manuelito has a strong will," Standing Bear replied quietly. "Stronger than any of the other headmen. He will die where he was meant to die. . .in Dinetah, the land of our Holy People."

When they arrived back at Fort Sumner, Terry made a written summation of their fruitless trip and it was sent to General Carleton at Santa Fe.

Carleton exploded in fury and vowed to take Manuelito dead or alive. However, such extreme action proved unnecessary. A report from Fort Wingate weeks later made General Carleton jump with joy and he rushed to Governor Connelly with the news.

"Manuelito has surrendered voluntarily at Fort Wingate!" Carleton said. "He suffered attacks by the Utes and Hopis and most of his warriors were killed. The others were too weak to fight and everyone was deprived of food and blankets!"

The governor chuckled. "So it was the Indians, not you, who forced him to surrender."

"We can all take the credit, but Manuelito had no choice. . .he was seriously wounded, losing the use of his left arm. He had only twenty-three followers with him when he dragged himself into Fort Wingate!"

CHAPTER THIRTY

"Drat those thieving Apaches and Mexicans!" Fort Sumner's post commander complained to one of his captains. "They've stolen most of the Indian's horses and just last night a band of Apaches made off with a herd of sheep! I want you to take a company of men and go after those renegades . . .those sheep must be returned, even if you have to kill the thieves!"

Terry volunteered to join the unit of soldiers, but Kit Carson stopped him. "You don't have to go," he said. "I can keep you here, if you want me to."

Terry shook his head. "I haven't been able to do a thing for these Indians, so far. . .if I can help get their sheep back, it's the least I can do!"

The group of soldiers started out in the dim light of morning, easily following a trail left by the stolen sheep. As the sun spread its gold across the prairie, nearly twenty rebel Apaches were spotted, grazing the herd of sheep in a shadowy hollow of land. The Indians caught sight of the soldiers and began racing their horses in escape.

"After them, men!" the Army captain shouted. "Don't let one of them get away!"

The company of soldiers spurred their horses forward in a wild chase and spread apart to encircle the fleeing Indians. There was a roaring gun battle between both Indians and white men while three Indians were killed and a few escaped into the hills.

During the melee, Terry didn't have a chance to shoot, for his horse took a bullet in the side and stumbled forward. Terry was thrown from the saddle and he looked up to see wild-eyed horses thundering toward him. All he could do was to throw his hands over his head and lie face down while sharp hooves trampled over his body.

One of the soldiers had been killed and Terry was placed, unconscious, alongside the man's body on a travois to be dragged behind his horse. The company returned slowly to Fort Sumner with the prisoners and all of the recaptured sheep.

Terry felt as though he were trapped under a deep sea of painful black water. When he finally rose to the surface and opened his eyes, Doctor Gwyther was staring down.

"You took a real beating, young man," the doctor said. "Everyone thought you had died with that other soldier. They even sent a report to the War Department about your death!"

Terry put a hand to his head and found it bandaged. At the same time, a lightning storm of pain raced through his entire body and he gasped.

"Don't fight it," Doctor Gwyther told him. "It'll be a few days before you get out of that bed!"

Terry closed his eyes and lapsed into another sleep, but this time it was from medication. When he awoke hours later, there was a terrible pain in his head and Doctor Gwyther gave him another pill, which helped only a little.

"How bad is it?" Terry asked.

"It's a miracle you weren't killed," the doctor said. "I've done all I could with the scant facilities here at Fort Sumner. As far as your leg is concerned, you'll be on crutches for a while."

"As far as my leg is concerned," Terry repeated. "You mean there's something else?"

Gwyther looked concerned. "You've also suffered a concussion. Only time can tell how you'll recover from that."

Terry vaguely recalled the doctor's earlier words.

"Do I remember correctly that you said a report of my death had been sent to the War Department?" Terry asked.

"That's right," the doctor replied. "I tried to stop it from going out, but I was too late. They sent a retraction, but the mail rider was killed by Indians, so they're sending another one."

Terry shook his head with worry. "Then, with all that delay, my parents will be told that I'm dead before the retraction gets through! I've got to send a letter to them right away and let them know I'm all right!"

Doctor Gwyther put a hand on Terry's shoulder. "Now, you just hold on. You're in no condition to do any letter writing right now. Your parents will get a correction soon."

When Terry was finally able to sit up in bed, he felt it urgent to let his parents and Susan Godfrey know he was alive. He had just finished a letter when Kit Carson paid him a visit.

"I tried t'see you earlier," Carson said, "but the Doc wouldn't let me. He says it'll be a spell before you're up and around again." Then he said, jokingly, "Glad you at least didn't hurt that writin' arm!"

"That's one good way to look at it," Terry replied with a grin.

Carson had a paper in his hand and gave it to Terry. "I got a reply from General Carleton and would be obliged if you'd read it to me."

Terry looked at the official letter and began reading:

"Your work has been admirable and it is only a matter of time before Bosque Redondo is a success. The main trouble, now, is raiding by Comanches on supply wagons coming from the east as they enter the Texas Panhandle. This situation must stop. Therefore, I cannot accept your resignation at this time but must give orders for you to go to the Panhandle with as big a force as we can muster and stamp out these depredations."

Kit Carson's face darkened as Terry read. Then the letter ended with one of General Carleton's sugar pills:

"However, after the long and hard campaign you have endured, you may visit your family for two weeks but must report to Fort Bascom and prepare for the campaign against the Comanches."

Terry handed the letter back to Carson who looked at it for a long moment. Terry wondered if he was trying to decide whether to stand up to Carleton or not. Then Carson choked in a cough and his face grimaced in pain.

"Are you all right, Kit?" Terry asked with concern.

Carson wiped his mouth with a handkerchief. "Jest a problem with my chest," he replied. "Had a horse fall on me a few years ago. Doctor said the aorta was injured, whatever that is. Sometimes it's kinda hard to breathe, is all."

"Are you going after the Comanches, like Carleton says?"

Carson's jaw muscles firmed. "If that's what the general wants me t'do," he said. "Cain't go agin orders and let my country down. But first, I'm gonna pay a visit home—the wife and children will be mighty happy to see me after all this time!"

Before Kit Carson left, Terry gave him the letters addressed to Terry's parents and Susan Godfrey.

"Would you do me a big favor, Kit, and give these to Fort Sumner's postal clerk. Please tell him they have to go out as soon as possible." He grinned ironically. "I'm telling my folks that I'm still alive. . .they think I was killed in that accident!"

"Be glad to," Carson replied, "but General Carleton's right about them Comanches. . .with all those attacks on the wagons and their damagin' the train tracks, the mail ain't gettin' through like it should."

Later in the day Terry's heart swelled when Standing Bear and Willow-

In-Storm came to see him. They were reserved in their words but Terry felt honored by their mere presence.

"Our people are grateful for your help in capturing the Apache thieves," Standing Bear said. "With our sheep returned, they can now be sheared and our women start making blankets."

"I really didn't do anything," Terry said in embarrassment. "All I did was get myself busted up!"

Willow-In-Storm looked at him gently. "We ask our spirits to bring back your health, Teri-O-Neel," she said. "You are one of the few with an open heart."

Her face showed a tenderness Terry had never seen before and he wanted to take her hand, but resisted the temptation.

"With good friends like you," he replied, "I ought to be on my feet in no time!"

Chapter Thirty-One

Kit Carson returned once more to his comfortable little home in Taos, but this time he was tired and his heart was heavy. The growing pressure in his chest prevented him from breathing easily at night and he did not look forward to another large campaign against the Indians. However, the sight of beautiful Josefa and the growing family brushed away any concern he might have carried with him from Fort Sumner.

There were five children, now, the latest being little Rebecca who was named after Josefa's mother. The others ran happily to greet their father.

"Papa! Papa!" they cried while Carson laughed and took small packages of goodies from his pockets.

"*Hijos*!" Josefa called from the doorway. "Let your Papa come in. . .you're as wild as the Indians in the hills!"

While the children tore open the packages and fought over their candy, Carson took Josefa in his arms for a warm embrace. Her eyes filled with tears as she pulled back to look at him.

"*Querido*," she said gently. "You are weary. . .come in and let me give you a decent meal. Then you can rest and be yourself again."

Kit Carson relaxed in the big chair always reserved for him on his visits. He held little Rebecca in his arms and it was not long before the older children were swarming around him, chatting noisily about their recent activities, while Josefa busied herself in the kitchen.

Finally Josefa called to them. "*Hijos*, let your father rest! And Teresina, help me here with your Papa's supper."

After the evening meal there was another reunion in front of the fireplace. Carson sat on the floor and his children gathered lovingly around him while he told them wild Indian stories. Josefa sat in the large chair with Rebecca in her lap, enjoying all the love that her husband had brought back into the home.

When the evening grew late, Josefa tried to send the children to their beds but was met with much arguing. Carson finally intervened and they went dutifully to their rooms. Josefa sighed in relief.

"They are becoming so unmanageable," she told her husband. "I wish you could be here all the time. They love you so much, they will do anything you tell them."

Carson put an arm around his wife. "I know it's hard on you. I think it'd be best if I built us a bigger house on that property in Colorado I bought from our good friend Thomas Boggs—he calls it 'Boggsville.' I'd feel better with you all livin' next to him."

"But you still would not be with us. I can tell in your eyes that you will be going away again. . .what is it this time?"

Carson kissed her on the cheek. "It's the Comanches. General Carleton wants me to stop 'em from raidin' the wagons in the Texas Panhandle."

Her face turned to worry. "Another fight with the Indians. Each time you do this, I sit at home wondering if I will ever see you again."

He hugged her body closer. "This'll be the last one, I promise. Then we'll all be happy in a big house in Colorado."

Josefa took the kerosene lamp and he followed her to their bedroom. Much later, they lay happily in each others arms, making up for all the lonely nights that had kept them apart. Josefa's eyes soon closed in relaxed comfort next to the reassuring presence of her husband. A moment later she heard him cough and he pulled himself away from her to sit up in bed.

"What is it, *Querido*?" she asked.

"Jest this pain in my chest," he replied. "When it comes on, I can breathe better if I sit up."

"A doctor should look at you!"

He ran his hand over her long black hair. "When I come back from Texas, I'll look up a doctor in Santa Fe or Albuquerque. Now, you jest git back to sleep and don't worry yer pretty little head. Everything's gonna be all right!"

She lay her head back onto the pillow but sleep was replaced with dread. That general in Santa Fe—Carleton was his name—was pushing her husband too far. He was no longer the young man he used to be, and now, his health was not good. In Josefa's heart, it was General Carleton who stood between her and her beloved husband.

She took his hand and closed her eyes. Maybe after this last campaign, he would break away and she would have Kit Carson as her own again.

CHAPTER THIRTY-TWO

Kit Carson stopped at Fort Sumner on his way to prepare for the Comanche campaign and went to visit Terry O'Neill in the post hospital. Doctor Gwyther had just finished an examination when Carson entered and Terry was sitting on his cot with a pair of crutches leaning against the wall.

"Well," Carson said amiably, "you 'bout ready t'start chasin' Indians?"

Terry beamed at seeing the colonel again. "I think that's going to have to wait a while—the doctor doesn't seem very happy the way things are going."

Doctor Gwyther shook his head in frustration. "They've stuck me out here with thousands of Indians and soldiers to treat and what do they give me to work with? Practically nothing! I've done all I can for Sergeant O'Neill, but his leg isn't healing the way it should and his headaches won't go away."

Terry tried to make light of the situation. "Maybe you oughta take me out and shoot me, doctor!"

Gwyther was not amused. "That's hardly the answer. But what I am going to do is recommend that you be sent back to the Army hospital in New York where they have specialists and the proper facilities."

"If you're gonna send him to New York," Carson said to the doctor, "it looks like Sergeant O'Neill's and my paths will be partin' fer good."

"I don't think he'll be coming back here," Gwyther replied. "I'm sure they'll give him a medical discharge." He walked to the door. "I'll leave you two to talk. I have to check on some medicine I ordered—which was six months ago!" He left the room in disgust.

"It just doesn't seem right, Kit," Terry said, "to send you against the Comanches, now, after all you've done. Please don't think I'm out of line by saying this, but I believe you've done more than what was expected of you. In my mind, I think General Carleton's been using you!"

Kit Carson bridled at the remark. "General Carleton's a fine military man! The general's loyal to his country and he's done everything he could to help it. I'm proud to serve under his command!"

Terry moved back on the bed with a sigh. "I'm sorry to feel that way, but it's just that the Indians once liked and trusted you. Now, the Navajos, especially, think of you as a traitor."

Kit Carson's steely eyes flashed. "I did what I thought was the only thing to bring the Indians and white men together in peace. I know a lot of those pore Indians died, but it jest had t'happen in a campaign sich as this."

Terry felt helpless. He knew it would be impossible to convince Kit Carson that he had been maneuvered into an ugly situation where Kit thought he was doing the right thing.

Carson took a deep breath and placed a friendly hand on Terry's shoulder. "Sorry I spoke so hard. I'm gonna quit this durned fightin' as soon as I'm through with them Comanches. I don't reckon we'll ever see each other agin, so I wanna say it's been good havin' you as a friend and helpin' with my letters."

Terry reached up and took Carson's hand in a farewell shake. "I think the greatest event in my life has been the privilege of knowing Kit Carson!"

CHAPTER THIRTY-THREE

The bandages were finally taken off and Terry moved from the hospital back into the barracks, but he was forced to use crutches. Also, the pain in his head kept plaguing him off and on. He kept writing letters but had not received any since his accident. He knew it was because of the marauding Comanches holding up the mail and that everyone back east thought he was dead. It would just take a while for the retraction to get through, but in the meantime, his heart ached for what his parents and Susan Godfrey must be feeling.

Terry stuffed the letters into his pocket and took a crutch under each arm to go to the mail room. When he stepped outside the barracks he saw that a large crowd of Navajos had just arrived and Deacon Jones was one of the soldiers lining them up for a count. Terry hobbled over to Deacon.

"Glad to see you got such a small group this time," Terry said. "I don't know how we can handle any more."

Deacon slung a rifle over his shoulder. "Oh, this is that bunch that escaped a while back. Most of 'em, anyway."

Terry was surprised. "You mean Barboncito?"

"Yeah, he's over there." Deacon pointed to one of the Indians.

The short thin Navajo headman sat with his people who were arranged in a line, squatting on the ground. Barboncito's face was grim and his coal-like eyes still held a look of defiance, but the slump of his body gave the appearance of utter defeat that made Terry feel sorry for the man.

"Where did they capture him?" Terry asked.

"Didn't have to," Deacon replied. "He and his people came in this mornin'. . .gave themselves up on their own.

"Almost everybody in the Territory has been chasing him," Terry said. "From the looks of him and his people, they must have been starved into surrender."

Terry limped slowly to the mail room and then made the crutches take him over to one of the cornfields where some of the Navajos were examining the tall stalks. There had been a problem with moths swarming through the fields and depositing their eggs, which developed into inch-long worms that hid under the husks to eat the kernels.

He saw Willow-In-Storm emerge from the field with some other Indians and he hobbled over to them.

"Is your corn going to be all right?" he asked the girl.

Willow-In-Storm shook her head sadly. "No. The worms have bored holes in the husks and let more insects get in. Every ear of corn is ruined . . .now, we have nothing!"

Terry shared her disappointment, knowing that the Indians had been depending on a good crop to supplement the meager rations of food from the government.

But it was only the beginning of their misfortune. That afternoon the sky grew dark with threatening black clouds and a heavy rain began, accompanied by gale-like winds that swept without mercy across the fields.

The storm raged for three days, while Terry and the others remained inside the barracks and the Indians shuddered in their little huts. When the sun finally came out, the Indians went to the fields again only to find their wheat pounded into ruin.

Soon, Doctor Gwyther was complaining to the post commander.

"I'm starting to get cases of malaria," Gwyther said. "Something has to be done about all those pools of stagnant rainwater in the reservation. Mosquitos are breeding like rabbits!"

The poor doctor handled the increasing load of patients as best he could and groaned in despair when a new group of Navajos arrived at the reservation, bringing with them cases of smallpox. A small epidemic broke out and soon many of the Indians died. Gwyther went again to the commander.

"My hospital is overcrowded with the sick and dying! Now, I've just learned that the Navajos are throwing their dead into the Pecos River! Do you realize what this is doing to the Apaches living downstream? They have to take their drinking water from a river full of maggots and rotting corpses!"

It was the last straw for the Apaches and during the night every last one fled the horrors of Bosque Redondo to return to the sanity of their own country.

The food problem raised its ugly head once again and many of the starving Navajo women turned to prostitution with Fort Sumner's personnel. One night Terry saw Deacon Jones with a cup of cornmeal he had stolen from the company kitchen.

"What are you going to do with that?" Terry asked.

Deacon grinned lustfully. "Givin' it to a pretty little thirteen-year-old Indian girl. Her mother told me I could sleep with her daughter if I'd give 'em some corn meal."

Deacon Jones eventually joined a host of other men infected with syphilis or gonorrhea that had become rampant and Doctor Gwyther's small hospital overflowed.

Terry was relieved to see that Standing Bear and Willow-In-Storm were miraculously spared of all the sickness. Although hunger preyed upon everyone, the old Indian counseled his people not to flee back to their homeland, lest they be hunted down and killed.

Space was at last available for Terry in the wagons going to Cheyenne and before leaving he went on his crutches to Standing Bear's hogan.

"It hurts me very much to leave you while the Bosque is in such a mess," Terry told the two Indians. "I wish there was something I could do."

"You have a good heart to think as you do," Standing Bear replied. "The other headmen and I are pushing your leaders to let us return to our homeland. With all the hunger and disease here, maybe this will happen soon."

Willow-In-Storm gazed at Terry with eyes full of sadness. "You have been a good friend, Teri-O-Neel," she said. "There will be an empty place in our hearts when you are gone."

Terry fought the urge to take her in his arms. Instead, he took her hand. She did not resist and her soft warmth flowed through his body.

"Knowing you has been the only sunlight in my clouded days here," he said. "I will never forget my wonderful Indian friends."

He turned quickly to hobble away before they could see the agony in his eyes.

CHAPTER THIRTY-FOUR

The orders from General Carleton to Colonel Kit Carson were short and to the point:

"I have given you more men than you asked for, because it is my desire that you give those Indians a severe drubbing. You know where to find them; you know what atrocities they have committed; you know how to punish them. Now, all the rest is left with you."

It was a cold mid-November day when Kit Carson arrived at Fort Bascom and he was happy to find his old friend Captain Jacob Riley waiting. They greeted each other warmly.

"When I heard the general was organizing this thing," Riley said, "I couldn't let you go into another battle without me!"

"Mighty kind of ye to volunteer," Carson replied. "Carleton's given me three hundred and thirty-five men and seventy-five Indians. With you along, too, we oughta make short work o' this fight!"

The large army of Cavalry, Infantry, scouts, supply wagons and two howitzers started out in the early morning while frost was still on the ground. The going was slow, due to the number of men on foot, plus the howitzers being drawn by pack mules, as the long line of men made their way northeast into hostile Indian territory.

Two Ute Indian scouts were sent far ahead each morning and they returned at dusk to report any sign of the enemy. Nothing was seen for the first few days, however the Ute and Indian scouts were becoming more eager the closer they got to their prey.

Captain Jacob Riley shared Kit Carson's tent and one night, after the Ute scouts had returned to camp, Riley was startled by the sound of thumping on the ground, accompanied by groans and howls. He looked through the tent flap to see Utes and Apaches stomping around the campfire. With faces raised to the dark sky, unearthly sounds erupted from their throats.

"What the devil are they up to?" Riley asked in puzzlement.

Carson chuckled. "That's their war dance. After all, they're on the warpath, now. Gonna fight their enemies, the Comanches and Kiowas!"

Jacob Riley was unable to sleep the rest of the night and tossed on his blanket while the strange sounds continued until dawn.

The war dance became a nightly ritual and there was nothing Captain Riley could do but get used to it. The group moved on, being held up two days by a snowstorm and, on the twelfth day, reached Mule Spring in the Texas Panhandle where they made camp. The particular day happened to be the second nationally established Thanksgiving Day, as designated by President Lincoln, but there was no celebration as the men steeled themselves for battle.

The two Indian scouts were sent out as usual and, while the camp waited their return, a fire was started in late afternoon for the evening meal. Jacob Riley was surprised to see all the Indians become alert at the same moment, then they stood facing east with hands shielding their eyes. Riley looked in the direction but saw nothing. Finally one of the Indians turned to Kit Carson.

"The scouts are returning," the man said.

Riley was astounded. "How do they know? I can't see a blasted thing out there!"

"That's why they're called scouts," Carson told him. "They got eyes better'n ours."

Riley kept staring for several minutes and finally spotted a pair of tiny specks on the flat plains. A moment later there was a faint shout from the distant riders and the Ute Indian turned again to Kit Carson.

"They find sign of many enemy," the man said.

Riley dropped the hand from over his eyes. "They know all that from just one little shout?"

The sighting was confirmed after the Utes rode into camp, however they refused to speak to anyone until they had gone directly to Kit Carson and made their report to the commander.

"As soon as it gets dark," Carson told Jacob Riley, "I'm takin' most of the men forward. Ye wanna go along?"

"I wouldn't miss it for anything!" Riley answered.

With only light from the stars, Carson and the other officers rode out with two hundred and fifty-nine men, leaving the howitzers to follow the next day. The group traveled eighteen miles and halted at midnight when the fresh trail of hostile Indians was discovered.

Kit Carson put a finger to his lips and waved an arm as the officers gathered around him quietly.

"Tell everybody no talkin' is allowed," Carson whispered. "And no lightin' of pipes or smokin'. They can dismount, but stand by their horses and hold the bridle reins."

Everyone stood the rest of the night, holding their horses' reins, while an early morning frost covered their faces. Captain Jacob Riley remembered the tragic cold of Canyon de Chelly and wished, now, he had stayed behind at the warm camp.

At the first sign of daylight, the group moved on and quickly found a village of at least one hundred and seventy tepees. The Indians, however, had seen the Army's advance and were fleeing on horseback while squaws and children ran for the bushes.

"Charge!" Kit Carson shouted.

The soldiers galloped forward with rifles drawn and began firing at the Indians as they raced for a nearby river. The redskins wheeled and fired back while more Indians came up from the rear.

Jacob Riley was amused to see that Carson's Ute and Apache scouts had all thrown off their clothing and covered themselves with paint and feathers, charging into battle. Not to be outdone, the enemy Comanches and Kiowas, also, were in war dress with their faces painted and feathered headdresses billowing in the wind.

As Carson's men pushed the hostiles back, another village of more than five hundred lodges was seen a mile behind. This, combined with the first village, made about seven hundred lodges.

"With two warriors to a lodge," Carson told Jacob Riley, "this means we'll be facin' nearly fourteen hundred Indians!"

It was clear that Carson's Army was outnumbered, however his rear guard arrived and the two howitzers were quickly put in place, aimed toward the enemy.

The gunner gave orders to fire: "Number one—Fire! Number two—Fire!"

As the cannons roared, one shell rammed completely through an Indian pony, pitching its rider forward. Two of his companions rode up and grabbed the fallen warrior by the arms, dragging him away to safety.

The hostile Indians were astonished at the howitzers' destructive force and turned their horses away, racing back to the distant village with prolonged yelping.

Kit Carson heaved a sigh of relief and looked around to survey the aftermath of battle. Two men were killed and several injured. One of them was Captain Jacob Riley who was lying beside his perspiring horse. Carson ran over to him.

"Jake, ye hit bad?" Carson asked as he knelt beside his friend.

"In the leg, dammit," Riley panted. "Can't get back on my durned horse!"

Not far away stood an old, deserted adobe building, once used as a trading post, and known to all frontiersmen as Adobe Walls. An area was set up inside where two Army doctors began taking care of Captain Riley, along with the other wounded soldiers.

A pall of quietness had now returned and Kit Carson ordered his men to unsaddle, water and stake their horses. Then everyone sat around to eat their breakfast of raw bacon and hardtack.

While Carson ate, he scoured the horizon through binoculars and was surprised to see, three miles east of Adobe Walls, another village of three hundred and fifty lodges. Even more jolting was the sight of at least one thousand Indians thundering on horseback toward his group.

"Git back on yer horses, men," Carson ordered. "We got another group comin' from the east!"

Almost before the men had time to resaddle, they were surrounded by a thousand screaming Kiowa Indians and the fighting started anew. Within the next few hours, additional Indians rode into the foray until almost three thousand Comanche, Apache, Arapahoe and Kiowa Indians were on the field at one time.

The battle lasted until late afternoon when Kit Carson saw his horses badly used up and supplies running low.

"We better try an' make it back to the supply wagon!" he said through gritted teeth. "Push 'em back as much as you can," he ordered his officers. "We'll retreat to the first village and destroy it, then find the supply wagon!"

But the Indians fighting in the rear had set fire to dry grass; the fire, spread by a brisk wind, raced toward the men. Carson brought his force together and moved to higher ground, then in retaliation, he set fire to the grass in front, the flames now raging all around them. The howling Indians galloped up to the dense smoke and flames, fired at their enemy through the conflagration, then rode back quickly.

After the fire had passed on toward the hostiles, Carson ordered a retreat and the Army rode back to the first village.

The Indians saw them coming and quickly went to work trying to save their belongings. The howitzers were brought up again and began firing until the Indians had been chased to one end of the village.

"Keep 'em at bay over there," Carson ordered one unit, "while we destroy the village!"

Soldiers quickly ransacked the lodges before setting them on fire; inside, they found plundered white women's and children's clothing, several photographs and a cavalry sergeant's hat.

Darkness had now fallen and the Indians were in retreat for the moment.

"They'll be regroupin'," Kit Carson told his officers. "We'll have t'git outta here durin' the night!"

Several campfires were started as a deception, making the Indians think Carson's men were at camp for the night. Then Captain Riley and the wounded men were loaded onto ammunition carts and gun carriages. The group began an ominous retreat in the darkness, hoping to find the supply wagon. Not only were they unsure of the exact position of the wagon, but the wounded were suffering severely, the men and horses completely worn out, also murderous Kiowas and Comanches lurked in the darkness.

No one spoke, although the crunching sound of the carts and carriages, along with moans of the wounded, would have alerted any hostile Indian that happened to be close. Nevertheless, the men trudged on in the dark, praying they were going in the right direction.

After three torturous hours, two campfires were seen flickering in the distance. Carson called a halt and wondered if it could be another Indian camp. He ordered two men to approach cautiously with their guns ready.

Everyone kept still, holding their breaths, while the men crawled on their bellies toward the campfires. Finally a voice called out.

"Halt! Who goes there?"

It was a sentinel at the supply wagon and the relieved men straggled into the camp for medical attention and a hot meal.

The battle at Adobe Walls was the biggest fight, in point of Indian strength, that ever occurred west of the Mississippi River. Due to the great number of Indians killed, General Carleton considered the campaign a success and that the redskins had been taught a lesson. He sent a message of congratulations to Kit Carson.

"Your fight was a brilliant victory," Carleton said. "It adds another green leaf to the laurel wreath which you have so nobly won in the service of your country!"

However, the words of praise were no consolation to Kit Carson. He knew he was outnumbered during the fight, which forced him to call a retreat; otherwise, none of his men would have come out alive. In Kit Carson's mind, he had suffered defeat by the Indians at the battle of Adobe Walls.

CHAPTER THIRTY-FIVE

Terry O'Neill had to laugh when he saw the horse-drawn army ambulance waiting for him at the New York train station. He was able to walk, although on one crutch, but he climbed into the vehicle, anyway, and was taken quickly to the military hospital.

"That doctor in New Mexico seems to have done a good job," one of the specialists said after examining Terry's leg. "But I'd still like to operate tomorrow morning and see if we can't get those bones in shape."

However, the other doctor, who had examined Terry's head wound, was skeptical. "If you're still having headaches," he said, "I'd like to consult an associate before giving a prognosis."

Terry had written of his approximate arrival at the New York hospital and waited eagerly to see if anybody would come visit. His heart sank when Tom and Clara O'Neill came into the room late afternoon the second day. His mother had changed very little—only her hair was a little whiter—but his father had aged considerably. He was frail and walked unsteadily with a hand on his wife's arm. Terry jumped up from a chair and hugged them.

"It's so wonderful to have you back with us," his mother cried, placing a loving kiss on Terry's cheek. "You can't imagine what we went through when they told us you were killed!"

"We just thank God it was a mistake," Tom O'Neill added. There was a weakness in his voice Terry didn't like.

"We took a room at a hotel nearby," his mother said." The Godfreys wanted us to stay with them, but you know your father."

"Come sit down, Papa," Terry said and helped his father to the chair. "You feeling all right?"

His mother answered while Tom O'Neill settled carefully into the chair. "Your father's rheumatism flared up not long after you went away. It's given him a hard time."

"Have you seen a doctor?" Terry asked with concern. "We have some good ones here."

"Oh, yes," his mother replied. "Two good ones here in New York. But they can't seem to help any."

Terry felt helpless and changed the subject. "Well, I've got a lot to tell you, but we have lots of time for that. They're operating on my leg tomorrow morning and the doctor says I'll have a few weeks of therapy."

His mother's brow wrinkled. "With your father's condition, we'd planned to go back to Monmouth this afternoon after seeing you." She looked worriedly at her husband. "Maybe we can stay another night?"

His father looked up with watery eyes. "Of course, we'll stay, Clara. I want to be sure Terry is all right."

Terry's throat tightened. "You don't have to stay over, Papa. I'll be all right, it's not a major operation. Why don't you two go on back home—I'll come for a long visit when they let me out of here."

Tom O'Neill shook his head. "No, no—I insist!"

Terry looked at his father with love. "Okay, but I want you to go back home right after the operation!" Then he gave his mother a puzzled look. "Speaking of the Godfreys, since they live right here in New York, I thought Susan would be the first one to visit."

His mother dabbed a happy tear from her eye. "We saw them right after we arrived in the city." Her smile changed slightly. "But I know Susan's dying to see you. . .she just probably wanted to give us a chance at you first!"

It was almost noon the next day when Terry came out of sedation but was not allowed visitors until the surgeon had consulted with his patient.

"Well, young man," the doctor beamed, "I believe we've got you back together as best we can."

"Just what does that mean?" Terry asked.

"The fractures were extensive and some bone particles had to be removed. But after therapy, I think you'll be able to walk. Remember, I said 'walk,' not 'run.' You'll need a cane, for a while."

A few minutes later, the specialist who had examined Terry's head injury came in.

"I'm told you'll be walking soon," the doctor said. "How's the head doing?"

"I still get these headaches," Terry said, "but not as frequent. . .maybe they'll go away altogether."

The doctor looked doubtful. "I'll be frank and tell you what we believe is giving you trouble."

Terry was apprehensive. "I want to know everything, doctor."

"The skull fracture you sustained may have caused a tumor to form. Of course, it's only a prognosis, but we've seen this same thing happen before."

"Can you operate?"

"With the location of injury, it would be risky. Oh, I could operate, but I wouldn't guarantee success. I'd need a signed authorization from you to allow the operation."

Terry swallowed dryly. "You mean. . .I could die?"

The doctor refused to say the word. "It's entirely up to you."

Terry shook his head in confusion. "And if I don't have the operation, what is my life expectancy?"

"I can only guess. If no tumor develops, you could live to a ripe old age."

"And if there is a tumor?"

"It's impossible to say for sure. You could have three. . . five years, maybe longer. There have been cases where tumors disappear, but that's very rare." He smiled gamely and patted Terry's shoulder. "I'll give you time to think about it. Just let me know when you've come to a decision."

Terry lay, staring at the ceiling, as the doctor started to leave.

"Wait!" Terry stopped him. "I'm going to take a chance at life. I don't want the operation."

The doctor paused at the door and turned back. "You're a brave young man."

"Dammit," Terry groaned. "I'm not brave. . .it's just something I have to do!"

Terry promised himself he would not tell anyone of the probable tumor; but then it wouldn't be fair to marry Susan, knowing they might have only a few years together.

When his parents were finally allowed to visit the following afternoon, he told them after therapy he would be walking soon and his head was all right.

"Now, please stop worrying and go back home," he urged them. "They're treating me well here and I'm happy as can be!"

Terry's spirits faded as soon as they left the hospital room; he was still bugged because Susan hadn't shown up.

The next morning, however, all the Godfreys arrived, including Susan, and the sun came back into his life. Both Susan and her mother gave him a kiss on the cheek and Sam Godfrey took Terry's hand in a gripping shake.

"That was quite a shock the Army gave us when they said you were dead!" Godfrey told him. "It'll certainly be good to have you back at the office again. I just bet you've got a lot of stories to write!"

"As a matter of fact, I have," Terry replied. "I've been lying here thinking about all that's happened to me and I really believe it would make a good series of articles."

"Good, good! Why don't you start writing them down now, while they're still fresh in your mind. I'll pop in every now and then and pick up your work!"

Mrs. Godfrey frowned. "Now don't rush the boy—he's just got out of the operating room!" Then she gave Terry a shy look. "Well, we've been doing all the talking. . .I think you and Susan would like to have a minute alone." She tugged her husband's arm. "Come on, Sam. We can wait in the lobby!"

After her parents left the room, Susan walked over to the bed and took Terry's hand.

"I'm so glad you're back. . .and alive," she told him softly. "I just know everything will work out for you."

Although her face had matured, she was still the pretty girl he remembered on the beautiful white horse so long ago. But, now, there seemed to be a veil between them—maybe it was what she said and how she said it that bothered him.

"I think you've changed a little," Terry said, then chuckled at himself. "I guess we both have—after all, it's been a few years, hasn't it?"

"It's been a while."

"Before we start making marriage plans, I have to tell you something. . ."

"Wait, Terry." She released his hand. "Let me say something first." She sat down on the foot of the bed with a strained look on her face. "Mother thought I should wait till you got out of the hospital, but I think you ought to know right now. . .I'm married, Terry!"

It was a long moment before he could reply. "Well, I think you're right . . .you shouldn't put off telling me something like that!"

She looked at him with eyes full of pain. "Terry, you've got to understand. . .they told me you were dead! I wanted to die, too. . .I would've killed myself if it weren't for my dear parents!"

He turned his head to the window. "Who's the lucky man? I guess he likes horses—he'd have to like horses."

She wiped tears from her eyes. "Yes, he was a captain in the Cavalry."

He didn't reply and kept staring out the window.

"But he was wounded in battle and got a medical discharge. He's employed with a law firm, now, here in the city."

Terry still couldn't find any words.

"He's a fine man, Terry. . .every bit as good as you. I know you'll like him. I'll bring him by so you two can meet."

He turned back to her with a stony expression. "That won't be necessary. I'll be busy with therapy and won't have time for visitors, anyway."

"Terry, I still love you. . .I've always loved you and wouldn't hurt you for anything in the world. . .it's just that when I thought you had died, I didn't have anything to live for. I was going out of my mind with loneliness! Then I met this wonderful captain. He made me feel alive again. He's really the one who saved my life." She sniffed into her handkerchief. "I was horrified after what I had done to learn you were still alive—but it was too late, then. Terry, if you hate me and never want to see me again, I'll understand."

He smiled grimly. "Don't worry about it, Susan. We'll always be friends. . .nobody can ever take that away."

She sighed with relief and kissed his forehead. "Oh, Terry, there's never been another man like you. . .and never will be!" Then she remembered what he had said previously. "Well, now, what is it you were going to tell me?"

He clenched his jaw. "Just that with me busted up like this and maybe being a cripple, it wouldn't be right for us to get married. So, it looks like you did the right thing, after all. I wish you a happy marriage, Susan."

"I love you, no matter what," she told him softly. "Your crippled leg wouldn't have made any difference." She gave him another gentle kiss and quietly left the room.

When he was alone again, he gritted his teeth to hold back tears of despair, not just because of Susan but because the way fate had thrown everything against him. He turned his face to the pillow and couldn't help it; the tears came anyway.

CHAPTER THIRTY-SIX

Pain stabbed Terry's head occasionally like a hot pitchfork and he tried to forget about it. Also, his leg did not respond as fast as the doctors hoped and the expected weeks of therapy turned into months. He forced himself to work harder each day, not only to bring his leg back into shape, but also to shut out the mental anguish.

Writing the articles kept his mind occupied and Sam Godfrey was elated with the stories. They were published in serial form with each edition eagerly snapped up by readers hungry for something other than tragic reports on the continuing War Between the States.

Whenever Sam Godfrey stopped by, he also brought along out-of-town newspapers so Terry could keep up with happenings in the west.

"One of these has a story about your friend Kit Carson's fight with the Indians," Sam said. "In the Texas Panhandle. . . place called Adobe Walls."

Terry scanned the article quickly and read that Kit Carson had been outnumbered and forced to retreat. "If I know old Kit," Terry sighed with regret, "that must have hurt his fighting pride to admit defeat!"

"The Army didn't look at it that way," Godfrey said. "Here's a later issue saying they made Carson Brevet Brigadier General of the First New Mexico Volunteers and allowed him to take a much-needed rest with his family at Taos."

December thirty-first arrived and crowds of revelers filled New York's streets to usher in 1865, hoping that the new year would bring an end to the terrible war. The next day, with a medical discharge, Terry left the hospital. He had to use a cane, but he was walking, and ready to face whatever the future had in store.

He took a train north to visit his parents, as promised, and his mother smothered him with affection when she met him at the station.

"Your father didn't feel up to meeting the train," she said. "Now that he's retired, it'll be nice having two men in the house!"

"Is he really that bad, Mama?"

Her look turned sad. "I'm afraid so. He found a buyer who paid good money for the gun shop. I'm just glad to have him home all the time, now."

When they walked into the comfortable little house Terry saw that his father had kept a good collection of rifles, all placed neatly in a gun rack by the front door. Tom O'Neill was in a comfortable chair with a blanket over his knees and Terry gave him a hug.

"Mother tells me now that you're retired, you don't have regular hours any more," Terry said.

Clara O'Neill answered for her husband. "With him home all the time, I'm trying to fatten him up!"

Terry took a gun from the rack and sighted down the barrel. "Maybe we can shoot a few birds while I'm here, Papa."

Terry saw a nostalgic look in his father's smile.

"I'm afraid my hunting days are over," Tom O'Neill said. "But you go ahead, if you want to."

Clara O'Neill went to the kitchen and started rattling around. "I've been waiting for you to come home so I could bake one of your favorite cakes," she said to Terry. "I picked some nice mountain strawberries just yesterday, we could have shortcake."

"That would be fine," Terry replied, "but don't try and fatten me up along with Papa!"

With the cane restricting him, Terry went hunting only once and brought back some quail. However, after two weeks of sitting around, eating his mother's wonderful cooking, he felt the itch to get back to New York. Besides, Sam Godfrey was waiting.

Tom O'Neill bade Terry goodbye and his mother reluctantly took him to the train station. Her eyes once again filled with tears.

"Now, I'll expect to see you again by the end of the year, Terry. You've always spent Christmas in New York with the Godfreys. . .we want you here with us for the holidays!"

Terry laughed as he hugged her goodbye. "All right, Mama, I promise . . .things are different, now."

The landlady at the apartment house in New York where Terry had previously stayed was overjoyed to let him once again have his original room, and Sam Godfrey beamed with pleasure when Terry returned to his old desk at Carper's Weekly.

"You've got to have dinner with us this Saturday," Godfrey said. "Susan and her husband will be there, it's about time you got acquainted!"

Terry had been trying to put that part of his life behind him and wished the Godfreys could understand. He made a feeble excuse and Sam Godfrey remembered what his wife had said was true—only time can heal a body's wounds.

Terry's leg improved over the following months until he was able to leave his cane at the apartment and walk stiffly to work and back. Each day he passed the park's riding stables and longed to be in the saddle again. The alluring smell of the stables finally became too much one afternoon and he went in. The groom was a young man he'd never seen before and his thoughts went immediately to Ben Adams and Rusty Rose.

"Lookin' for a ride?" the groom asked.

Terry looked around at the familiar barn and was pleased to see it had changed little. "I used to ride a horse here called Rusty Rose. Wonder if you have another one like her?"

The groom thought for a moment. "Can't say as I remember a horse by that name—but, then, I've only been here 'bout a year."

"Well, I would like a ride. You see, I have a bad leg, so it'd have to be a gentle horse."

The groom went to the barn and led out a pretty sorrel. "This one here's called Storm Willow," he said. "But don't let the name throw you, she's 'bout as gentle as you can find."

The name gave Terry a jolt and Willow-In-Storm's pretty face leaped into his mind. "I think that's the one for me!"

The groom threw on a saddle and cinched it up, then helped Terry onto the horse. Terry winced with pain as he threw the right leg over, then relaxed in the saddle and felt good again. He ran his fingers through Storm Willow's mane and the animal turned her head to size up its rider. Terry coaxed the horse forward and they began a slow trot down the path that took them through trees stretching overhead like welcoming green arms. Terry's mind rolled back to the times when he and Susan had ridden this same path. He felt a small ache in his heart and knew he shouldn't have come here. It was no good reliving old memories and he turned the horse around.

"You're a good horse, Storm Willow," he told the mare. "No reflection on you, but I think we'd better go back, now."

As he rode into the stable area, two other riders had just returned; one was a young girl and she noticed Terry with a surprised, happy expression.

"Terry O'Neill!" she called. "Is that really you?"

Terry saw that it was Susan Godfrey and he cursed himself for coming to the stables. He forced a smile. "None other," he replied lamely.

The groom led her horse away and she walked quickly over to Terry. "My, you're looking good," she remarked, staring up at him.

"Thanks—and you're as pretty as ever!"

It was impolite to stay in the saddle while they talked and he wanted to get down, but knew it was impossible without the groom's help.

"That's my husband over there," Susan continued. "I think it's time you two met!" She turned and called to the man who had just dismounted. "Charles, come here. . .I want you to meet a good friend!"

The thirtyish-looking man walked over with a friendly smile. He wore riding pants with a large brown coat that had long, full sleeves.

"Terry O'Neill," Susan said, "this is that wonderful man I told you about who swept me off my feet. . .Charles Middleton!"

Terry reached down and they shook hands.

"Pleased to meet you," Terry said. "I work for Susan's father at Carper's Weekly."

Charles Middleton's face broke into a mixture of surprise and chagrin. "Why, of course, Susan's told me about you. . .you two were engaged at one time." Then he changed to grim embarrassment. "I truly regret the way things turned out, Terry. I can't blame you if you harbor any ill feelings."

It was Terry's turn to feel embarrassed. "Oh, there's no hard feelings. It's just the way life is, sometimes."

Charles tried to break the mood. "I've been reading your articles in Carper's Weekly. . .they're really smashing!"

"Smashing?" Terry couldn't help saying.

Susan laughed. "Never mind the way Charles talks. . .his parents are from England."

Charles looked abashed. "I must say I was born here in New York, but with my parents being British, I suppose I couldn't help picking up a bit of their speaking habits."

"Are you just starting out," Susan asked Terry, "or have you finished your ride?"

Terry was afraid the groom would come over to help him down and he didn't want them to witness the spectacle.

"Well. . ." he started to say, but his fears came true when the groom appeared out of nowhere with an outstretched hand.

"Here, mister," the boy said, "I'll help you down so you won't hurt that leg!"

Terry gritted his teeth, not only from embarrassment but also from agony, as he pulled the right leg over the saddle and was eased to the ground with the groom's help. As the horse was led away, Terry stood in pain, knowing that he wouldn't be able to take a step without the dratted cane, which was back at the apartment.

Susan looked at his stricken face. "Terry, are you all right?"

He gave her a crooked smile. "Just this blasted leg. I never should've tried to get back on a horse so soon."

"Are you able to walk?"

"After it limbers up, I'll be fine."

"Here, let us help," Charles said while he and Susan each took one of Terry's arms. "Our buggy's just over there. Please, let us give you a ride wherever you're going."

Terry was at their mercy, but wondered what he would have done if they hadn't come along. They helped him to the street and into their buggy.

"My apartment's just a few blocks down that street," Terry pointed. "I'm really obliged for your help."

While Charles started the horse forward, Susan studied Terry with compassion. "Terry, why don't you have dinner with us at Mama and Daddy's house? We get together every Saturday night. Daddy sees you every day, but Mama's been dying to see you again!"

Charles glanced at Terry. "Do say yes, Terry, I'd love to hear more about your adventures in the west!"

There seemed to be no way out and Terry caved in. "Well, I suppose I could get away," he replied.

Susan clapped her hands in glee. "Wonderful! We'll pick you up, then . . .say around six?"

The following Saturday, Susan and Charles delivered Terry to the Godfrey residence and he suddenly felt like a stranger. The place had always been a second home to him, but now everything was different and he entered the house with hesitation.

Mrs. Godfrey received him with a warm hug and took his coat, then Charles Middleton removed his coat. Terry was shocked to see that Charles' left shirt sleeve was pinned up. He was missing an arm. All this time the man had been using only his right arm, but Terry never realized it.

They settled themselves in the parlor's comfortable overstuffed chairs while Sam Godfrey poured bourbon for the men.

"First of all," Charles said to Terry, "I want to hear how you injured your leg. . .I understand you were chasing Indians!"

Susan frowned. "And then I suppose you'll tell him how you lost your arm! I don't want to hear all those gruesome war stories!"

Terry leaned forward with interest. "On the contrary, Charles, just how did it happen?"

Charles sipped his drink. "In deference to Susan, let's just say it was during the battle at Williams Ferry. I was lucky to get out alive, believe you me. Simply in the wrong place at the wrong time and took the brunt of a cannon shot."

"Well, that's one way to get out of the Army," Terry said, trying to make light of the unpleasant subject. "With me, they just didn't want somebody who can't get on or off a horse anymore!"

After a wonderful dinner they sat before a cheery fire and nursed brandy from large, round crystal goblets while Terry was urged to tell of his life with the Indians.

He told them of his meeting with the strong-willed Manuelito who distrusted the white man, and also about the friendship of dignified Standing Bear and his stubborn but beautiful niece; but when he came to the suffering at Bosque Redondo, Terry paused.

"If I go on," he said, "it'll just make you cry. Why don't you wait and read about it in my next articles!"

It was late when Susan and Charles delivered Terry back to his apartment and they parted with vows to get together again soon.

When Terry retired for the night, he almost ignored the pain in his leg as he lifted it up onto the bed. The resentment festering inside was gone, now; he was pleased with Susan's husband and glad to see her so happy. He wondered if he would ever be as happy again.

The growing friendship with Susan and Charles Middleton gave Terry a new life and he threw himself into his work at Carper's Weekly. He was writing at his desk one afternoon with renewed fervor when Sam Godfrey burst into the office.

"News just came in!" he shouted with a beaming face. "General Robert E. Lee has surrendered at Appomattox. . .the war is over!"

Terry leaned back in his chair with relief and thanked God that all the killing had stopped.

"I want you to join us at the house tonight for a champagne celebration!" Godfrey added.

Susan and Charles were at the Godfreys, also, and after they drank to peace between the states, Charles proposed another toast.

"Now I want us to raise our glasses to another historical event," he announced with pride and lifted his glass. "Susan and I would like you all to drink to the expected new member of the Charles Middleton household!"

There was a round of happy congratulations and everyone took another sip of champagne.

Mrs. Godfrey thrilled at the prospect of becoming a grandmother.

"Have you decided on a name yet?" she asked Susan and began to think. "Let's see, there's your grandfather William. . .or maybe his wife Elizabeth, she was a wonderful woman. . ."

Susan laughed. "We won't need your help, Mother. Charles and I have already decided, but we want to keep it a secret till the baby arrives."

Mrs. Godfrey looked playfully hurt. "How can you do this to your own mother, Susan. Why, I'll be on needles and pins!"

CHAPTER THIRTY-SEVEN

"You'll never believe who's in the lobby to see you," one of the women clerks told Terry O'Neill in his office.

He looked up with curiosity. "Who is it?"

"Says his name is General Christopher Carson!"

Terry dropped his pencil and rushed to the lobby. Sure enough, that same, familiar short man with the gray-streaked hair, rusty moustache and slight stoop was waiting with a smile.

"Kit!" Terry exclaimed and grabbed Carson's hand. "I heard your were in the east, but I didn't think there was a chance we'd see each other!"

"Thought it'd be downright sinful not to stop by an' say hello when I was this close," Carson replied. He looked down at Terry's leg. "Looks like they fixed you up all right."

Terry laughed. "It's fine. I just have a limp, now, is all."

"I've been followin' yer articles," Carson said. "You're doin' right good with 'em."

"Well, you're a celebrity around here. . .and there's someone at Carper's Weekly who'd kill me if I didn't introduce you!" Terry took Carson by the arm. "Come with me."

Terry ushered Carson to Sam Godfrey's office, knocked on the door and then took Carson inside. Godfrey looked up through his glasses.

"Sam Godfrey," Terry said with pride, "I'd like you to meet the man we've been writing about all these months. . .General Kit Carson!"

Godfrey's mouth fell open and he got up to take Carson's hand with hesitance. "Is this some kind of joke?"

"No joke," Terry said. "This really is my good friend Kit Carson!"

Sam Godfrey recovered quickly and the three sat down for a friendly chat.

"While you're in New York," Godfrey said, "my wife and I would be honored if you could have dinner with us. . .and my daughter and her husband would be thrilled to meet you!"

"I planned to jest spend the night," Carson told him. "I'm takin' the train back west tomorrow mornin'."

"Then it'll have to be this evening," Godfrey said. "We won't take 'no' for an answer. . .Terry and I will pick you up at the hotel at six!"

Mrs. Godfrey, on short notice, turned out a delightful dinner. While they ate, conversation turned to Kit Carson's recent peace treaties with the Apaches, Comanches and Kiowas.

"That must have been difficult to arrange," Sam Godfrey said, "after the Sand Creek massacre last year. I understand the Indians are still angry!"

Mrs. Godfrey looked up from her plate. "I don't keep up with the world like I should—what was the Sand Creek massacre?"

"There was a colonel named John Chivington," Carson said, "who ordered his troops to destroy a Cheyenne village."

"They were living peacefully," Godfrey added. "Flying both the American and white flag. The soldiers murdered them in cold blood, women and children too. They say the poor Indians were even mutilated."

Mrs. Godfrey shuddered. "Well, I hope we can all live in peace, now, without any more of this killing!"

"I know there's those that don't agree with me," Carson said, "but I think the reservation plan is the only hope fer peace with the Indians. Take the Navajos. The rich ones with lots o' cattle want t'live in peace, but then there's the poor ones who are the majority, with no head chiefs, and live only by robbin' for food. If they're left scattered all over their land, the Mexicans will jest keep on robbin' from 'em, as well.

Susan and Charles Middleton had been listening with riveting concern.

"Do you think the Indians will agree to a reservation plan?" Charles asked.

"If we don't get 'em together and help 'em," Carson told him, "they'll die out soon from three things—their own wars between themselves, venereal disease introduced by the white man and intoxicatin' liquor, also provided by the white man."

Susan was full of sympathy. "Now that the peace treaties have been signed, I wonder if all the poor Indians will survive."

Kit Carson graced her with his sad blue-gray eyes. "The only thing I can say, ma'am, is I believe, now, they at least have a good chance."

When Sam Godfrey and Terry took Kit Carson to the train station the next day, they all shook hands in farewell and Carson put a hand on Terry's shoulder.

"I'm right proud of you, boy," he said. "You come a long way from jest writin' letters fer a tired old colonel back in New Mexico!"

Terry glanced down in embarrassment. "Thank you, Kit. You take care, now. . .maybe I'll be able to write another letter for you one of these days."

Terry and Sam Godfrey waved while Carson boarded the train. As it moved slowly down the tracks, Terry felt a renewed esteem for Kit Carson, as if their two lives were somehow parallel; but there was another side to the tired enigmatic man that Terry would never understand.

CHAPTER THIRTY-EIGHT

"What a beautiful place!" Josefa cried with delight and looked around Fort Garland in southern Colorado. "I am so happy you agreed to be the post commander."

"Thought I oughta have you and the children live with me here," Kit Carson said to his loving wife. "I've been leavin' you all alone too much."

It was a pleasant fortress with attractive buildings of rough adobe and logs chinked with mud, sitting high above the San Luis Valley, commanding a spectacular view of heavily forested mountains rising one upon the other to a crown of snow-crusted peaks.

The self-contained establishment had everything Josefa would need— a laundry, bakery, tailor shop, storehouse, sutler's store and even the fort's own chapel. Fresh clear water was always at hand with containers at each corner of the parade ground supplying cold water from the mountain snows. The officers' quarters had even the luxury of board floors and whitewashed walls.

Josefa gave her husband a warm hug. "The Army may still have you in its grasp, *Querido*, but at least my family will be together, now. It does not matter that this is not even our real home."

The unruly Carson children quickly took it as their home and became a familiar part of Fort Garland as they ran squealing like wild, untrained mustangs around the establishment. Josefa was further pleased that her husband had ample time to play with the children and was once again among his Indian friends.

The Ute Indian Chief Ouray, or "The Arrow," was Kit Carson's close acquaintance from years back. Ouray and his people lived in the outlying hills and when they learned that "Father Kit," who had once been their Indian agent, was at Fort Garland, the Indians streamed in, asking for food and care.

Kit Carson squatted on the ground with them, talking in the Ute language of sign and pantomime, while Chief Ouray listened with a stoic face.

"I'll give you what food we can spare," Carson told Chief Ouray, "as long as we can all live in peace. My soldiers here at the fort tell me some of your people are still raiding the settlements."

"That is true," Ouray replied. "But they follow words of other chiefs. I cannot control them."

"One of the white men's big chiefs is coming to Fort Garland next week," Carson advised. "His name is General Sherman. He wants to speak with you about stopping the raids."

"I will speak with him," Ouray said, "but I cannot make promises."

When the wiry but congenial General Sherman arrived, he was given a room in the officers' quarters and went to confer with Kit Carson. As he and Carson sat talking, the children ran half-clad and boisterous through the room, with two-year-old Rebecca jumping into her father's lap.

General Sherman smiled at the warm family atmosphere and asked, "What are you doing about your children's education, Kit?"

Carson looked concerned. "I've had practically no education, myself," he replied, "and I know I haven't done right by my children, lettin' 'em run wild like this."

The general thought a moment. "I received a scholarship at the college in South Bend, Indiana. Why don't you let me share it with two of your boys for, say, five years each?"

"Why, thank you, General," Carson replied. "I'll talk it over with Josefa."

When the Ute Chief Ouray arrived to talk with General Sherman in Kit Carson's office it was an impressive scene. Carson sat behind his deerskin-covered desk next to a gun rack made of deer hoofs while the mounted head of an elk looked down from above a burning fireplace. General Sherman sat, puffing on his brier pipe and Chief Ouray was shown into the room.

The chief was formally dressed for the occasion in painted deerskins and beaded moccasins. His sleek ebony braids were tied at the ends with silver ornaments and he carried a peace pipe that was intricately decorated. He spoke in guttural tones with an abundance of hand signs while Carson interpreted.

"The people in my camp live in peace," the chief said. "I have told Father Kit that I am not in control of those under other chiefs."

General Sherman answered. "The white chiefs think everyone would live in peace if all the Utes would settle on a reservation."

"That may be good," Ouray said. "But my people would not consider such a thing unless our enemies, the Comanches and Cheyennes, agree first."

Carson turned to General Sherman. "You can argue all you want to, General, but he's gonna hold to that."

The general tried another avenue. "But what about the raids by your people. . .can we come to some kind of agreement on stopping that?"

Carson translated the general's words to Ouray and the chief replied, "Those in my camp will do what I say. But we will have to bring together all the other tribal chiefs and talk peace with them."

"Can you arrange that?" Sherman asked.

"I will gather as many as I can to come to the fort in seven days," Ouray told him. "Now, we will smoke peace pipe between you and those in my camp."

The chief lit his peace pipe, took a puff and passed it to Kit Carson. Carson drew on the pipe and issued a cloud of white smoke. Then he gave the pipe to General Sherman. The general removed his own brier and put the peace pipe into his mouth. He pulled in a small amount of smoke and suppressed a frown. The choice of tobacco was not the best.

Governor Cummings and General Rusling were invited to attend the discussion and, on the seventh day, as promised, Ouray and the other tribal chiefs came to the fort. With them were almost all of their people, for over three hundred white wigwams were set up in front of Fort Garland in symmetrical blocks, like a city with streets. Squaws dressed themselves in glittering beaded clothing with bright feathers while the men wore a multitude of dress, from old army uniforms to narrow breech cloths. The atmosphere was like a country festival and soldiers from the fort mingled with the Indians to barter for souvenirs, which they would take with them back east.

When the council finally began, Kit Carson, the governor and General Rusling joined the tribal chiefs, all sitting on the ground in a circle. The peace pipe was lit and passed around, however General Sherman preferred to smoke his own brier while pacing back and forth with hands stuffed into his pockets.

Chief Ouray and his principal warrior Shavano, or "Blue Flower," presided and were intelligent statesmen. Kit Carson spoke volumes with them in their own language, at times giving General Sherman a translation.

"We must find a way to live in peace with the white man," Ouray told the chiefs.

An old Indian replied, "But the white men use the Indians' land and kill the Indians' food.

"Tell them we will control that," General Sherman said, "if they promise to stop raiding and killing."

It took many long hours with much talk and hand signing, but at last a compromise was reached and the chiefs all made their mark on a treaty.

Adhering to Indian custom, presents were exchanged and in the afternoon, three prize cattle were roasted with everyone taking part in the feast of friendship.

Generals Sherman and Rusling, together with the governor, left Fort Garland the next day, tired from the celebrations but filled with satisfaction.

Soon after they had departed, Josefa planned a small celebration for her husband's birthday, but on the day before, she went into labor with her next child. Carson summoned the post surgeon who shooed the children out of the house and by late afternoon, Josefa had presented her husband with another daughter. Josefa named her Estafana.

"That's a big name fer sich a little girl," Carson said jokingly. "I'll jest call her 'Stella.'" Then he became serious. "Maybe we oughten to have any more children. I git jest plain wore out playin' with all the ones we got now!"

Kit Carson's health had been a growing concern for Josefa.

"I think your position here is too much for you," she told him. "I am still waiting for the day when you will take us all to the new house at Boggsville. . .do you think perhaps that time has come?"

He looked at her with a weary sigh and kissed her cheek. "You always had the wise head in the family, Chipita. Maybe I oughta put in my resignation."

Josefa hugged her newborn daughter with happy relief. At last the dream was coming true—her husband would be free of the Army and she would have the family together permanently in their own home.

CHAPTER THIRTY-NINE

"Now, don't forget," Susan Middleton chided Terry in mid-December, "we're expecting you to be with us again at mother and daddy's house for Christmas!"

He had to disappoint them, however, for he vowed to honor the promise to his mother that he would spend the holidays with his parents. He took the train north and there was a light snow on the ground when he arrived at the modest little house in Monmouth.

"We're almost like celebrities in this little town," his mother told him happily. "Everybody's reading your articles and they all know you're our son—we're so proud of you!"

"Now that I can get along without that cane," Terry said, "why don't I go out and get us something for dinner? I'm itching to do some hunting like Papa and I used to."

"You do anything you want, son. This is your holiday as well as ours!"

Terry bundled up in a big coat, took a gun from the rack and stuffed shells into a pocket.

"Be careful," his mother called as he left the house. "And don't stay out too long. It'll be dark in another hour or so!"

The weather was brisk and his breath clouded as Terry crunched through the firm ground toward a slope behind the house.

There were tracks in the snow and Terry followed them to a thicket. He saw a movement in the bushes and a white rabbit jumped out, running. Terry quickly raised his gun and brought the rabbit down with one shot. He put it into a sack tied to his belt and trudged on. Soon, another rabbit jumped out in front of him and he brought his gun up fast but the familiar pain suddenly jabbed his head like a hot knife. He jerked the trigger and the gun roared, but the rabbit kept running. He cursed and plodded on. He would have to get two rabbits for their dinner.

It was getting dark, when Terry returned to the back of the house where he skinned and dressed two fat rabbits. His mother baked them, along with mashed potatoes, vegetables and a homemade apple pie for their dinner.

That night, Terry lay in his bed, happy to be home again, but he worried about his father's poor health. If he were taken away, Terry wondered what would happen to his mother. Suddenly the headache returned and he clenched his fists until it vanished. With final relief, he was able to sleep.

Terry awoke the next morning, expecting to hear his mother rattling around in the kitchen, preparing a large breakfast, but the house was silent. He put on a robe and went to the living room. The only light came from his parents' bedroom door. He peeked in to see his father on his knees at the bedside.

"What is it, Papa?" Terry asked with trepidation and walked into the bedroom.

Then he saw his mother's face, marble-white, lying motionless on the pillow. His father's thin body trembled with quiet little sobs.

Clara O'Neill's funeral was a simple affair with a small crowd of local friends gathered at the tiny cemetery just outside Monmouth. Tom O'Neill was totally crushed by his wife's untimely death and when he and Terry returned to the lonely house, Terry fixed a simple dinner. While the two sat, with no appetite, Terry looked at his father's grief-stricken face.

"Papa," he said, "I have to go back to New York, but I can't leave you here alone. Why don't you come with me. . .we could share my apartment in the city."

Tom O'Neill shook his head. "No, son, you have your own life with the Godfreys and everybody. I'd never fit in."

"Of course you would. . .and the Godfreys would love to have there with them."

His father had stopped trying to eat. "It's just that with your Mama gone, now, there isn't any reason for me hangin' around."

"That's not true. You have a lot to live for."

"We loved each other so much. Now, all her caring for me, putting up with me, is gone. It's like I've lost everything!"

Terry's jaw firmed. "When I was in the hospital, I didn't know if I'd ever walk again. Then I found out the girl I loved had married someone else. On top of that, they told me I had a terminal brain tumor. I thought I'd lost everything, too, and wanted to die, just like you!"

His father looked surprised.

"But I stopped thinking about myself," Terry continued, "and decided to grab every day that's left and make the most of it! And you know something? I found out there was a lot of love waiting for me out there!"

His father's eyes glazed. "You never said anything about a tumor."

"I didn't want to worry you or Mama. It was my problem and I was determined to live with it."

Tom O'Neill gave a tired sigh. "You're a brave boy, and I'm proud of you, son. But don't you see—my body is wasting away with pain so bad sometimes I don't think I can stand it. Now, with Clara gone, there's no reason to grab those days that are left for me."

Terry's eyes moistened and he felt helpless to continue the argument. He looked at their uneaten dinners. "Well, looks like neither of us is hungry, I'll clean up the kitchen. Why don't you go sit down and we'll talk about this in the morning—you'll feel better then."

His father got up from the table. "I'll go out on the porch and smoke my pipe."

Terry called after him, "Please, Papa, think about coming back to New York with me."

When Terry finished with the dishes, he went to join his father on the porch and saw that a rifle was missing from the gun rack. A cold dread rushed through him and he went outside to see his father sitting on the porch steps with the gun barrel at his head. Terry froze in the doorway, afraid to move.

"Papa, don't!"

His father looked up with baleful eyes. "I want you to know I'm proud of you, son. . .really proud!"

Terry's eyes filled with tears. "Papa, you always lived by the gun. . .please don't die by it, too!"

The gun went off with a blast that made Terry squeeze his eyes in horror and the terrible sound echoed through the hills. When he looked again, his body went limp in anguish.

"Papa!" he cried.

Tom O'Neill lay at the foot of the steps; a new snowfall had begun and the flakes were melting quickly on a pool of warm blood forming around his body.

Chapter Forty

With an aching heart, Terry returned to New York and found that Susan and Charles Middleton had become parents two days earlier. She and the baby were alone in the hospital room when he came to visit.

"Oh, Terry," she cried, "you don't know how crushed I was when I heard about your parents. That must have been a terrible blow. . .I'm so sorry for you!"

"Thanks," Terry replied. "At least I know they're both happy, now." He looked down at the bundle in her arms. "Well, now, is this the new little Middleton?"

"Just look at my little girl," she said happily and pulled a corner of the soft blanket away from the baby's face.

Terry bent down for a look. "Can't say she looks like you."

Susan laughed. "All babies look alike at first. Give her a few months."

"Now, just what is that secret name you had for her?"

"Charles and I decided that if it were a boy, we'd call him Terence, after you."

Terry raised up in embarrassment. "Well, then, I'm glad it wasn't a boy."

"And, we decided if it were a girl, we'd call her Teresa."

He sighed in defeat. "I guess there's no escape. . .but why in the world did you want to name your child after me?!"

"First, because you're our best friend."

"And second?"

She became serious. "Charles always felt guilty marrying me while you were away. . .and so did I. He knew how much you loved me and that you must have been terribly hurt. He was proud of the way you accepted everything. We both admire you, Terry. It seemed only right to name our baby after you."

Terry felt smothered by warm gratitude. "Then, I'm deeply honored!" He bent down to kiss Susan lightly on the forehead.

CHAPTER FORTY-ONE

The new house at Boggsville had not been constructed yet, but Kit Carson moved his family into a comfortable home next door to the trading post run by John Hough. Josefa could stand in her doorway, which was lined with pine, and look west at the outlines of the Spanish Peaks and the Las Animas River rushing not far away.

Although her husband was not in good health, she rejoiced, for he was no longer badgered by the military and she had the family back together again. Remembering his words about not having more children, she smiled ruefully at her growing stomach; they were expecting another one in April.

The children, now a collection of six, ran with excitement to meet their father as he came from the trading post.

"Papa! Papa!" they cried and took hold of his legs, almost dragging him down.

It pained Josefa to see her husband's thin body and gray hair as he doled out the expected sweet tidbits and patted the younger ones' heads. He walked to the doorway and she wrapped an arm around him for a welcome kiss.

But the sunshine in Josefa's heart was soon to be darkened by a letter that her husband had picked up at the trading post. He took it from his pocket and handed it to her.

"It's from General Carleton," he said. "John Hough read it for me."

She took the letter as if it were tainted.

"I won't read it, *Querido!*" she cried in fear. "I refuse to read it!"

Carson smiled at her. "It's the Utes agin. Old Chief Ouray's got some complaints and wants to go to Washington for peace talks."

"But what do they want of you?" Josefa demanded.

"Since Ouray and me are such good friends, the commissioner of Indian Affairs thinks it'd be a good idea if I was there, too."

She pulled him close and her tears spilled onto his shoulder. "Please, my *Querido*, tell this General Carleton that you can no longer do his bidding . . .that you are too ill for such a long journey!"

He smoothed her silky dark hair. "I'll go to Santa Fe and talk with the general. We'll see what can be done."

The cheery morning sun found General Carleton pacing his office floor in Santa Fe with a feeling that the world was closing in.

The citizens of New Mexico were blaming him for raids by some of the hold-out Navajos, saying that the Indians were from Carleton's Bosque Redondo reservation; the demand for beef, wheat and corn to feed the Indians had raised prices all over the Territory, and Superintendent of Indian Affairs Michael Steck continued with his diatribes against the conditions at the Bosque, calling them deplorable.

Even the newspapers were writing unkindly editorials, stating that New Mexico was bringing Indians from Arizona to feed, and there were rumors of a whispering campaign in Washington against General Carleton.

When Kit Carson arrived, the general greeted him with a dark smile.

"I'm counting on you to go to Washington with me and the others," Carleton said. "Not only to make the Utes sign a treaty, but to help stop all these negative things being said about me."

"Josefa doesn't want me to go," Carson told him. "She thinks I'm too sick to make the trip."

Carleton gave a hearty laugh. "Why, you never looked better!" he said.

It was a conniving remark, for the general was disheartened at Kit Carson's frail body and the dull eyes that used to carry the bite of cold steel.

"And besides," Carleton added, "there are much better doctors in the east—you could look them up while you're there."

Carson pondered a moment. "I'll have to give it some thought."

General Carleton moved quickly to another tactic. "You've no doubt heard of all those newspaper remarks against Bosque Redondo. When you return from Washington, I also want you to go back to the reservation and whip that place into shape!"

Carson looked up with a new spark in his eyes. "I've done all I can for Bosque Redondo," he said quietly. "If I decide to go to Washington, when I git back, Josefa and me and the children are gonna settle down at Boggsville and let everything else go to the devil!"

The general was taken aback at Kit Carson's defiance.

"But, Kit," he replied soothingly, "I'm in a bad situation with all this negative attitude going around. . .you're the only real friend I have who can help!"

"Look, General," Carson said evenly, "I've carried out all yer orders—done more'n I ought to, maybe. Everything I did was what I thought the country needed to bring peace in the Territory. Now, I'm through. I'm tired and I want to spend the rest o' my days with my family." He sighed heavily in resignation. "All right, I'll go to Washington, but it's only because the Indians need me and are expectin' me to help 'em. And it'll also be the last one of yer orders I'll follow!"

When Kit Carson returned to Boggsville and told Josefa of his decision, tears of disappointment rolled down her cheeks.

"But you can't go," she cried. "It will be too hard on you!"

"I really oughta be there, Chipita. They're dependin' on me to help the Indians. If I don't go, I'd be lettin' everybody down."

"But what about this illness? I cry at night to see how it troubles you to breathe!"

"There's a lot of specialists back east that could maybe help," he said. "Ain't that, alone, worth the trip?"

CHAPTER FORTY-TWO

The office in Washington was filled with military and government officials, along with Chief Ouray and his Ute headmen. The Indian chief expressed his grievance and Kit Carson translated the words.

"We signed your treaty in good faith at Fort Garland with Father Kit and General Sherman," the chief told them. "But the white men still come onto our land and rob us of our way of life."

Kit Carson interpreted the white officials' reply.

"The only way to keep the peace is to protect your people on a reservation," General Sherman said. "We will settle you on a vast amount of land in western Colorado, from the White River on the north to the Rio de Los Pinos on the south."

The Utes discussed the offer with doubts.

"And what protection does the white man give us on this reservation?" Chief Ouray asked.

"We promise that no one, except agents, officers and government men, can enter, reside, pass over or settle upon the confines of this reservation."

The Indians could only rely upon the white man's promise and, after much haggling, agreed to sign the proposal.

After the meeting, on their way back to the house where the conference members were staying, Kit Carson appeared discouraged.

"You don't look satisfied with the treaty," General Fremont, Carson's long-time friend, said. "It was the only thing we could do."

"That treaty was worthless before the ink was even dry," Carson replied. "I've seen it all before. Settlers will still be comin' in to rape the Indians' land and there ain't nothin' we can do to stop 'em."

General Fremont was distressed to see his good friend so frail with illness and knew Carson was going on to New York to consult with a doctor there.

"I'll send word to my wife Jessie to meet you during your stay in New York," Fremont said. "If you need anything, she'll be only too happy to help."

Jessie Fremont left word at New York's Metropolitan Hotel where Kit

Carson would be staying; he was to let her know when he arrived and she could come see him. But instead, Kit Carson went to her own home to visit.

"Kit!" she admonished him. "You're in no condition to be running around the city, I was going to come to you!"

Carson chuckled lightly. "I couldn't let you do that. I am still alive!"

However, he was so weak he had to sit down in order to make conversation.

"I've already seen the doctor, here, but he couldn't do anything," Carson told Jessie Fremont. "The Ute Indians wanted to be with me on the return west, so I have them now in my hotel room. I told the doctor if he could jest help me take the Indians back where I can die with my own people, I'd be obliged."

Jessie Fremont choked back her tears. "Kit, you must let me help in some way."

"Thanks, Jessie," Carson replied, "but the chiefs and me are goin' on to Boston tomorrow to see another doctor. Then we're goin' straight home. If I died here, it would kill my wife!"

Josefa's child was due at any time, but she insisted on having Tom Boggs drive her in the buggy to meet her husband's stage when it arrived at La Junta, just north of Boggsville.

Carson's eyes softened with love when he saw his beautiful wife so burdened with pregnancy.

"Chipita, you needn't have come to git me!" He kissed her cheek.

"I had to come," she told him. "I have been so worried ever since you left. . .please, don't ever leave me again!"

Josefa suffered the bumpy ride in pained discomfort as Tom Boggs drove them back the short distance to their home. The children greeted their father with wild screams of delight and he finally had to order them to play quietly outside while Josefa retired wearily to her bed. Carson knelt beside his wife and lovingly stroked her raven hair.

"This is gonna be our last child," he told her.

She smiled up at him. "It will be another girl this time."

He was amused at her usual sage predictions. "And how do you know, little one?"

"It does not beat me with its fists. . .only your sons have done that."

It was early evening when John Hough's wife Ramulda was called to assist Josefa in giving birth to a healthy baby girl. While the child was being carefully washed Carson laid a cool wet cloth on his wife's forehead.

"I always let you name the babies," he told her, "but this time, I already got a name picked."

She was too weak to answer and only looked at him with questioning black eyes.

"You insisted on naming a boy after me," he continued, "so, with this last one, I'm namin' her after you. She'll be called Josefita."

Kit Carson was too ill to sit up with his wife, so Ramulda Hough stayed for the next few days. Even in his ill health, Kit Carson was happy, but on the tenth evening Mrs. Hough came to him with heart-stabbing news.

"Your wife has closed her eyes peacefully," she said with tears on her cheeks. "But she will never open them again."

CHAPTER FORTY-THREE

General Carleton looked with scorn at the Weekly New Mexican's latest issue that lay on his desk and he read the editorial once more with growing anger:

"Carleton has so long lorded it amongst us and done so little to win gratitude of our people, or the confidence of the War Department, that he has gained the detestation and contempt of almost the entire population of the Territory."

An adjutant stuck his head through the office door. "Governor Connelly's here to see you, sir."

Carleton stifled his irritation. "Then show him in."

Governor Connelly entered with a dour look on his face and Carleton rose to shake his hand.

"Please sit down, Governor," Carleton said. "I'm sure this morning's newspaper is what brings you here."

"That and President Johnson's reaction to the charges against you by the New Mexico legislators," Connelly answered with scorn.

Carleton frowned "I'm not surprised that the president is upset. After General Sherman's visit to Bosque Redondo, the report he took back to Washington was unfavorable."

"Unfavorable is an understatement! If I recall his words correctly, General Sherman told the president that 'the once proud Navajos have sunk into a condition of absolute poverty and despair.'"

"Well, unfortunately, General Sherman came at a bad time," Carleton hedged.

"There has never been a 'good time' at Bosque Redondo! And then you played a wrong card by preventing the superintendent of Indian Affairs from talking peace with the Apaches in Arizona Territory. . .I heard this morning that Michael Steck has resigned in disgust over your policies."

"I'm aware of that," Carleton said, "but it's good riddance. At least he'll no longer be around to stir up trouble!"

"And also, President Johnson is sending General Pope here to examine the Indian problems in New Mexico. I can assure you that he's not going to like what he finds!"

The governor's face was now dark with condemnation and Carleton felt as though a hot blanket had been stretched over his head.

Connelly's parting words were laden with bitterness. "I'm sorry I ever listened to you from the beginning. I can see my ship going down, and my only consolation is that when it does, yours will go with it!"

The new post commander at Fort Sumner received an urgent message from General Carleton to spruce up Bosque Redondo and make it look as favorable as possible for General Pope's visit. But what could the helpless commander do? The place was a mess and there was nothing that could be done in such a short time.

General Pope arrived in New Mexico to find the Bosque Redondo reservation a deplorable hovel of ragged and starving humanity. Then he went to Santa Fe where hardly anyone had a kind word for General Carleton's policies. Michael Steck's replacement, Superintendent of Indian Affairs A. B. Norton, added fuel with his urgent plea to relocate the Navajos on a reservation in their own country.

General Pope took his briefcase, bulging with negative reports, back to Washington and it was not long before the results hit New Mexico like a cleansing tornado.

A dark cloud hovered over Santa Fe's Palace of Governors as Governor Connelly read the classified government order. He was not surprised to learn that he and three important Territorial officials were to be replaced. Connelly's career was at an end, but his face took on a wicked smile, knowing that General Carleton was holding the same message.

Not far away, Carleton slumped in his chair as he read the official order from Washington:

"General James H. Carleton is hereby asked to resign as head of the Department of New Mexico and will report to Washington for further assignment."

Chapter Forty-Four

Bosque Redondo buzzed with the news that officials from Washington were arriving to talk with the Navajo tribal leaders.

Standing Bear's spirits brightened. "Perhaps, now, we will have a chance to make them see why we must be allowed to return to our Dinetah," he told his niece.

Willow-In-Storm's heart swelled with a precarious joy.

"The others will want you to speak to them," she replied. "I know they will listen this time!"

When the Washington officials and top military men gathered in a meeting room at Fort Sumner, they greeted the Navajo leaders politely, but with concern.

"We have been told many things from many people about this reservation and have, ourselves, seen Bosque Redondo for what it is," General Sherman told the Indians. "Now, we have come together to hear what you have to say."

Standing Bear stood up before the determined old Manuelito and other tribal leaders.

"I have been chosen to speak for our people," Standing Bear told the white men. "Since arriving on the Pecos, the Navajos, as you call us, have been constantly hungry and our sheep decimated. The soil here is not Navajo ground and refused to accept our plantings. Our crops did not flourish but withered and died. The Comanches, whom we have never known before, attacked and robbed us. Our people died, not only from hunger, but also from diseases that were new to us. We beg to be returned to our own country. Even if we starve there, we will have no complaints." Standing Bear's last words were steeped in despair.

"What does the government want us to do, more than we have done? Or more than we are doing?"

The Indians had now placed their fate as a last resort into the hands of the white man. Only time would let them know if they would ever see their beloved Dinetah again.

CHAPTER FORTY-FIVE

Agonizing pain struck again and Terry O'Neill held his head tightly with both hands, wishing he could squeeze out the deadly thing growing inside. When relief finally came, he breathed heavily and came to a decision that had been nagging him for weeks.

Susan and Charles Middleton's little girl was standing up, holding onto a chair, when she saw Terry come in and the delighted child plopped onto the floor with arms outstretched.

"Teresa!" Terry said as he raised the child high above his head. "You're getting to be such a big girl, I can hardly lift you anymore!"

"I do believe that baby loves you as much as her own daddy," Susan told him while stirring a pot of soup on the stove. "I wish you would come by more often."

Terry sat down with Teresa on his knee. "Well, I'm afraid you won't be seeing me for a while," he said.

Susan stopped moving the large spoon around and looked at him. "What do you mean?"

"I'm going back to New Mexico."

"Not for good, I hope!"

"Maybe so."

She frowned. "Oh, Terry, why do you want to leave us? We're all just like one big family!"

Terry bounced the child on his knee while she gurgled with pleasure. "The Indian situation's coming to a head, now, and I'll have only a few more articles to write. Thought it might be a good idea to be there when they call it quits. Besides, Kit Carson's very ill and I'd like to see him again."

"Well, Charles will be home any minute," Susan pouted. "When he hears the news, I guess you know you'll have ruined our dinner!"

It was a blustery morning when Susan and Charles drove Terry in their buggy to the train station. Little Teresa was like a China doll in a brown coat and fur collar with her flaxen hair tied up in a blue ribbon. Terry gave the child a last affectionate hug, then Charles took Terry's hand in a strong shake.

"It's going to be lonely in this city without you," Charles said.

"You ought to come with me and get away from all this noise and smoke," Terry said. "With New Mexico growing so fast, I'm sure they could use another good lawyer."

"Don't tempt me," Charles laughed, "I just may take you up on that!"

Susan wrapped her arms around Terry and her eyes filled with tears. "I told myself I wasn't going to cry." She kissed him lovingly.

The train whistle sounded and the porter waved to them. Terry released Susan and picked up his bag. "I'll write to let you know my address."

He climbed up the steps of the pullman and raised an arm in farewell as the train began to move away. He knew he would never see his friends again and watched with loving eyes as they slowly dwindled to small figures on the station platform.

CHAPTER FORTY-SIX

Terry O'Neill purchased a gray horse in Santa Fe and rode seventy miles to the northeast until he had passed through acres of chamisa bushes and bright-yellow daisies into a thirty-mile-long canyon. Rising gloriously in the west, the Sangre de Cristo Mountains made good their name of Christ's Blood with a mantle of snow that was bathed in the orange colors of a morning sun.

It was a cool April morning when Terry rode into the little town of Taos. The crisp invigorating air was penetrated by an occasional squeal of the two-wheel oxcarts bringing in peas, beans, eggs, pumpkins, apples, peaches and grapes to sell in the open-air market that took up a large area of the central plaza. The relaxing quaintness of Taos was irresistible and Terry could see why Kit Carson had chosen the idyllic town as his home.

Terry had assumed that a person of Kit Carson's repute would be easily found and the first produce seller happily gave Terry directions to the Carson family home.

Terry followed one of the narrow streets that spread from the main plaza, past unassuming little adobe buildings huddling together as if for warmth, until he arrived at a plain earth-brown house with wooden beams stretching over the facade.

An old Mexican man with a faded serape thrown over his shoulder stood by the front door. He held a tattered straw basket and was strewing seed for the chickens cackling and scratching at his feet when Terry rode up.

"Excuse me, *Señor*," Terry said and pushed back his dark hat. "Is this the home of Kit Carson?"

The man looked up with a big moustache that lifted in a friendly smile. "*Sí*, that is correct."

"I'd like to visit with him. I'm an old friend who has come a long way."

The Mexican's moustache drooped. "Oh, I am sorry. *Señor* Carson is not here. He and his wife go to stay in new home at place called Boggsville in Colorado, close to Fort Lyon."

Terry was disappointed. "Do you know if Kit Carson's health is improving?"

The Mexican looked even sadder. "No, he is very sick man. And his wife, I hear she die only two days ago while giving birth. . .but the baby girl, she is all right."

Before leaving Taos, Terry stopped at a local cantina for a *cerveza* to sustain him on the journey north.

"You're a stranger here," the Mexican bartender said. "Just passing through?"

"I'm going to Boggsville to visit an old friend," Terry replied.

"Boggsville? You must be planning to see either *Señor* Boggs or General Kit Carson—but the general is not there."

Terry was disheartened. "But I was told he has a new home there!"

"That is true, but he is so ill, a good doctor friend has taken the general to stay with him at Fort Lyon."

Fort Lyon, in Colorado, was one of the rudest and dreariest posts on the western frontier. Like most western forts, the establishment was unenclosed. Grouped about a sun-baked parade ground, the buildings had roofs made of long boards that were untrimmed, their ends creating irregular overhanging eaves.

When Terry O'Neill rode into the establishment he went to the sutler's store for information. The owner was behind the counter talking with a customer when Terry entered and they turned to see the newcomer.

"Good morning," Terry said. "I'm looking for General Kit Carson. Could someone tell me where he's staying?"

"Perhaps I can help you," the customer said. He was a medium-built man with a little goatee and round glasses, wearing a dark coat over gray trousers. "I'm Doctor Tilton, the post surgeon and also the general's doctor."

Terry shook the doctor's hand.

"My name's Terry O'Neill. Kit Carson and I are old friends. We served together during the Apache and Navajo campaigns. I was sorry to learn that he's seriously ill and I've come from New York to see him."

Doctor Tilton sized Terry up quickly. "General Carson isn't receiving visitors, but if you're an old friend who's come all the way from New York, maybe he'll make an exception."

"Just how ill is he, doctor?"

"The general suffered an injury years ago that weakened the aorta and caused an aneurism to develop. The growing pressure is causing spasms in his bronchial tubes."

Terry was bewildered by the medical language. "Will he recover?"

The doctor shook his head sadly. "There's nothing we can do but wait for the aneurism to burst—and that'll be it."

A tragic pang shot through Terry's heart. "Is he conscious. . .would he know me?"

Doctor Tilton chuckled. "Oh, yes, indeed. Like an old moose that's been wounded and won't fall down till the bitter end! He's staying at my house. Come along, I'll take you there."

Officers' row was composed of small houses fashioned from rough stone blocks chinked with mud. Each home contained four rooms and floors of unfinished lumber. Wooden partitions between the rooms were eight or nine feet high, with the remaining space to the rafters filled in with flour sacking.

The dreary facade of Doctor Tilton's house belied its cozy interior when he and Terry entered. A small blaze in the fireplace lent a warm glow over the main room and another man rose from his chair to greet them. Doctor Tilton introduced him.

"Terry O'Neill, this is a long-time friend of the general's, Mister Scheurich from Taos."

Terry and the man shook hands.

"I ran into Mr. O'Neill at the sutler's," Doctor Tilton explained. "He's an old friend, come from New York to see the general."

"Pleased to meet you," Mr. Scheurich said. "I'm married to Kit Carson's niece. He made me godfather to his children years ago, and now his wife's given me one more to see to!"

A familiar voice came from beyond the partition. "Did I hear the name O'Neill?"

Doctor Tilton led Terry into another room where Kit Carson lay on the floor among a pile of blankets. He was covered with a buffalo robe with his head propped up on a pillow against the wall.

"I know you've given strict orders not to see anyone," Doctor Tilton said, "but I've just met this young man who's come a great distance to see you. His name is Terry O'Neill—says he's an old friend."

Kit Carson stirred under the buffalo robe and extended his right hand. "Terry O'Neill! Don't tell me you came all the way out here jest t'see a sick old man!"

Terry shook Carson's hand warmly. "I came to see a good friend," he replied."

"Sit down, sit down. . .Doctor, please find him a chair."

Doctor Tilton pulled a chair over and Terry seated himself.

"Hate fer you t'find me like this," Carson said. "I'd be in a bed, but I can breathe better sittin' up here on the floor."

"When I stopped in Taos, they told me about your wife," Terry said gently. "I was very sorry to hear about it."

Kit Carson's once-sharp eyes were now a bleary gray. "Well, maybe it was fer the best, since I ain't got long, myself. My good friend, Scheurich, is gonna have his hands full, now, with them seven children!"

"I've read everything I could on what's been happening out here."

"You still writin' articles about all this?"

"That's right, I am."

"Well, thar's been a lot happenin', all right. You heard, o'course, General Carleton got run out." Carson heaved a sigh. "The Bosque jest didn't turn out the way he'd planned. If it hadn't been fer ever'body fightin' him hand and foot, and then all that disease and crop failures, I really think it'd have worked out."

"But look at all the death and misery it left behind. I'd think General Carleton, and everyone else involved, would have some remorse about the whole thing."

A spark of defiance lit up Carson's dull-gray eyes.

"It's men like that dog Colonel Chivington who massacreed them Indians at Sand Creek that oughta feel remorse! Whoever heerd of sich doin's among Christians! The pore Indians had our flag flyin' over 'em. . . that same old stars and stripes we all love and honor. . .thought they'd be safe. Well, then here come along that durned Chivington and his cusses. They'd bin out several days huntin' hostile Indians and couldn't find none no whar, and if they had, they'd run from them, you bet! So they jest pitched into these friendlies and massacreed 'em! Yes, sir, literally massacreed 'em in cold blood, in spite of our flag thar. . .women and little children, even! Why, witnesses saw Chivington's men shoot down squaws and blow the brains out of little innocent children. . .even pistoled little babies in the arms of their dead mothers, and worse than that! And you call these civilized men Christians? And then call the Indians savages, do you?" Carson thumped a finger on Terry's foot. "I tell you, I never laid a finger or pulled a gun on any squaw or papoose, or killed an Indian man who wasn't ready t'kill me!"

Carson squinted in pain and coughed into a handkerchief. He looked at the red stain and then up to the doctor. "It's blood," he said.

"Do you want some chloroform?" Doctor Tilton asked.

Carson waved his hand. "No, it ain't that bad this time." Then he explained to Terry, "Doc Tilton gives me chloroform when my breathin' gets t'hurtin' so bad I cain't stand it." He tapped his chest. "If it warnt fer this, I might live t'be a hundred years old!"

Carson made himself comfortable again and got back to the subject.

"Yes, a lot o' them pore Indians died at the Bosque, but that ain't the way I planned it, either. I hear now, they're lettin' the Navajos go back to their own land under a peace treaty. Looks like all the hell ever'body went through was fer nothin'!"

"No," Terry said, "it wasn't for nothing. I used to be like everyone else, thinking the Indians were of no consequence. Now, because of all this turmoil, everyone has been shown that the Indians are a people with their own culture and beliefs. We're all human, no matter what our color or creeds are."

"I was hopin' I'd live t'see the day when we'd all be livin' in peace," Carson replied quietly. "Looks like, now, I ain't gonna make it." His face became a grimace of pain and he coughed into the handkerchief again. "Doc," he gasped. "Guess I better have that chloroform, after all!"

Terry got up from the chair. "I'll let you rest, now, Kit. I'll come back tomorrow." He patted Carson's shoulder. "No matter how the others may look at all this, I'll always think of Kit Carson as the greatest Westerner of all!"

Terry left the room while Doctor Tilton administered the anesthetic.

The post commander, General Penrose, was able to find a place for Terry to spend the night and next morning Terry went to Doctor Tilton's house. The doctor was just coming out when Terry arrived.

"I'm afraid the general's gone," the doctor said. "The aneurism burst last evening and he suffocated in his own blood."

Although Terry had been expecting it, the news still formed a knot in his stomach. "I'm sorry to hear it," he said. "Is there anything I can do?"

"Thank you, no," the doctor told him. "I'm just on my way to tell General Penrose, he'll take care of things here at the post. Mr. Scheurich and I can handle everything else."

"The funeral will be held here, I suppose?"

"Yes, but the general's body will be taken immediately to Boggsville for burial next to his wife. Eventually, at General Carson's request, the two will be laid to rest at the cemetery in Taos."

The post flag was lowered to half mast and all troops off duty were ordered to attend the ten o'clock funeral, conducted by "Holy Joe" Collins, the post chaplain.

General Kit Carson's body lay in a rough pine casket that was lined with a white wedding dress, graciously donated by the wife of Captain Casey, and the coffin was decorated with the only flowers that could be found—white paper ones from the women's hats.

While Terry stood among the small crowd, three fifers and three drummers from the Infantry played a somber march. Terry's mind went back to an article he'd once written about a meeting between Kit Carson, General Sherman and General Rusling at Fort Garland in Colorado.

Rusling had been very impressed with Kit Carson, stating that, "his eyes were mild and blue, the very type of good nature, while his voice was soft and sympathetic. A man of rare kindliness and charity, such as a truly brave man ought to be—as simple as a child, but brave as a lion. Kit Carson took my heart by storm."

Terry felt much older now, and perhaps a little wiser, but would never comprehend the simple, yet complicated, man who was being carried by military escort to the gravesite in Boggsville.

With all the death and suffering that followed Kit Carson, there were many who hated him with no forgiveness; but Terry knew that a person of Carson's stature would have to carry a certain amount of regret with him to the grave.

Three volleys were fired by the Cavalry and three by the Infantry while the Napoleon guns of the fort sounded each minute during the simple service. After taps was played, a muffled drum roll provided the final salute to General Christopher Carson.

CHAPTER FORTY-SEVEN

Before leaving Fort Lyon, Terry O'Neill looked up Doctor Tilton to say goodbye. As they talked, Terry's face grimaced in pain and he put a hand to his head. The doctor studied him with interest.

"That must be some headache," Tilton remarked.

"The Army doctors say it's a tumor," Terry gasped and then sighed with relief as the pain vanished. "It all started when I got trampled by some horses."

"Brain tumor is a tricky thing to deal with!"

"Is that one of your specialties, Doctor?"

"Never went into that field, but I've read quite a lot on the subject."

"I know it'll get the best of me one of these days," Terry said with resignation. "Trouble is I don't know when that day will come along."

"From what I know about brain tumors, the pain will become more frequent toward the end."

"I just don't want to suffer."

"You might be lucky. . .so to speak. Sometimes the patient merely blacks out and dies in his sleep."

Terry chuckled grimly. "Well, that's a comforting thought. And there's nothing that can be done for a brain tumor, they say."

Doctor Tilton shook his head sadly. "I'm afraid that's true."

Terry went back to Santa Fe and took a room where he wrote the Kit Carson article, then sent it off to Sam Godfrey in New York; but he had one last story to write.

It was a sunny June day when he rode into Fort Sumner and was struck by a rush of emotions as he gazed upon its buildings and the sad Indian hogans at Bosque Redondo. He rode over to the one where Standing Bear and Willow-In-Storm lived, wondering if they had survived all the Bosque's horrors.

The old Indian had seen Terry's horse and came out of the hogan. Standing Bear's face did not break into a smile, but his eyes couldn't mask the pleasure of seeing Terry again.

"You have come back at a good time," the Indian said as Terry dismounted and tied the reins to a stake.

"I hear you're going back to your own land and I am glad," Terry said.

Willow-In-Storm peered through the doorway and then stepped out into the sun. She fairly glowed at seeing Terry once more.

"You have come to say goodbye again, Teri-O-Neel?"

The sight of her smooth tan face like windblown sand, and the way she spoke his name, made him realize that she had been in his heart all this time.

"I come to wish you happiness," Terry said. "But I hope it's not goodbye—I plan to live here in your country, now."

Her face warmed in pleasure. "That will only add to our happiness!"

Standing Bear wrapped a blanket around his shoulders. "I am going, now, with Manuelito and the other headmen to sign the peace treaty with the white chiefs," he said. "Do you wish to come with us?"

"Yes, very much," Terry replied and went with Standing Bear to Fort Sumner's meeting room.

Several Washington officials, together with General Sherman and other high-ranking Army officers were there, along with the important Indian leaders. Terry listened as the peace terms were read aloud.

If the Navajos returned home, the government would draw a boundary and the Navajos would not be permitted to cross that line except to trade. The government would give them each a number of sheep and issue weekly rations of food. The Navajos must live at peace and must not fight, even with other Indians. If trouble occurred, it would be reported to the nearest military post. In the future, the Army would do the fighting. No Navajos would be allowed to raid the Ute Indians; however, if the Utes or Apaches came into their country they could drive them out. The choice as to the location was up to the Navajos; the government would remove them either to the Indian Territory in Oklahoma or back to their own country. Ten leaders would be selected to stand responsible for the actions of their people.

Of course, going to Oklahoma was out of the question and the Navajos signed the treaty, providing that they be returned to their original land.

Terry and Standing Bear went back to the hogan with news that the government was arranging for the Navajos to be returned to their own country.

"I'd like to remain here until you leave," Terry told them, "so I can write it into my last article."

"Where will you stay?" Willow-In-Storm asked. "Here at the fort?"

Terry's forehead wrinkled. "I'm not sure. They may not have room for me, with all the government men here."

Standing Bear waved his hand at their hogan. "You are welcome to stay with us."

Terry glanced at the small structure. "Thank you, but I don't think you have room for me to lay down another blanket."

Willow-In-Storm's eyes grew soft. "I will be happy to share my blanket with you."

Terry looked at Standing Bear with embarrassment, but the old man's face remained expressionless.

"Well, if it's all right with your uncle," Terry replied.

The night was balmy with a half moon casting silver beams over Bosque Redondo and the Navajos began putting out their fires before retiring. Standing Bear wrapped a blanket around his shoulders and grumbled slightly as he lay down in the hogan. Before taking off his clothes, Terry looked at the Indian with hesitation, but the old man had turned his back and was soon breathing easily.

Terry removed his clothing and sat down beside Willow-In-Storm who raised the blanket from her naked body. She gave him a tiny smile of welcome and he lay down beside her. As their bodies came together, the touch of her smooth, light-bronze skin sent a tingle through him like the faint crackles of lightning in a fresh desert storm.

She melted into his arms and suddenly everything seemed to make sense, for this was the real reason he had come back to New Mexico. With all the suffering that had wracked his soul, this simple act of giving one's self to another—unselfishly and with love—washed away all barriers and recriminations.

Chapter Forty-Eight

The morning sun bathed Bosque Redondo in a gentle warm glow as Terry and Willow-In-Storm awoke, resting blissfully in each other's arms.

The cheerful day was quickly shattered, however, by rumors of a terrible incident that stunned the Indians and they saw their hopes teeter on the edge of doom. Terry went quickly to the fort headquarters to investigate.

"Lieutenant Jordan's detachment found the bodies of four men, murdered by Navajos," one of the soldiers told Terry.

Terry was dumbfounded. "Are you sure it was Navajos?"

"They were floating face downward in the waters of Twelve Mile Creek," the man said. "Two Navajo arrows and three bullet wounds were in the first body, with the head cut by an axe. The second body had been shot by four arrows and the third man's feet were tied with a rope. That one had four Navajo arrows in his chest plus another axe wound to the face. There were two arrows in the stomach of the last one. His face was cut by an axe, too."

Terry went back to the hogan in dejection and explained the dread incident to Standing Bear and Willow-In-Storm.

"We were so close to Dinetah," the girl said and tears welled in her eyes. "This is because there are still those who wish to keep on killing. . .will it ever end?"

General Sherman was in Santa Fe, preparing to return to the east, when he received the report. He angrily ordered Fort Sumner's commander, General Roberts, to call together all the tribal leaders.

"The general will not be satisfied of your good faith under the peace treaty," the commander told the Indians, "unless the guilty Indians are turned over to the authorities."

"We are aware of this terrible thing," Standing Bear said, "and have found that the murderers are Navajos who fled Bosque Redondo weeks ago. We have their names and can tell you in which direction they ran."

A large force of soldiers took with them an Indian who would recognize the killers and they went after the renegade Navajos.

A blanket of tense silence spread over Bosque Redondo as the Indians wondered if they would ever see their beloved Dinetah again.

Terry had finished washing himself in the morning when Willow-In-Storm came to him and took his hand.

"Come with me, Teri-O-Neel," she said. "The men are performing the coyote ceremony today."

He was puzzled. "What's a coyote ceremony?"

"Our spirits will speak through the coyote and tell us which direction we are to take."

Terry followed the girl to a clearing where her uncle and the Navajo men stood in a large circle. A gray-brown coyote waited in the center, warily looking around with strange empty eyes. Terry thought perhaps it had been partially sedated with a particular herb or weed that the Navajo medicine men used.

Standing Bear walked over to the coyote, bent down and opened its jaws. The scraggly animal did not resist while the old Indian placed a small, round turquoise stone in its mouth. Then Standing Bear stepped back and everyone waited in tense silence while the coyote held the stone on its tongue and walked slowly around the circle of men. Finally, it paused for a moment, then turned and walked unwaveringly toward the west. The men stepped aside to let the animal pass.

A murmur of happy relief sprang from the Indians and Willow-In-Storm put her hands to her face.

"The coyote tells us we will be going west!" she exclaimed tearfully. "To our Dinetah!"

Soon the renegade Navajos were brought back to the fort. They had been found sleeping in a gully and were captured after a furious battle in which two Indians were killed.

"We wish that these men be punished for their crimes," Standing Bear said, "for we cannot allow any threat to our return home!"

On the final night before the Indians' departure, Terry O'Neill and Willow-In-Storm lay on the blanket, giving of themselves completely, for this was to be their last time together. Her uncle snored gently in the darkness not far away.

"Teri-O-Neel," Willow-In-Storm murmured when they had caught their breath, "after tomorrow, am I never to see you again?"

The thought of saying goodbye cut through him like a saber, for he had fallen deeply in love with the beautiful girl.

"I plan to live in Santa Fe. We won't be too far apart." He kissed her forehead.

"There is no need for us to live apart. You could come with us. . .we would have our own hogan and be together like this forever."

The idea startled him at first. Then he remembered that Kit Carson lived with the Indians for eight years; there was no better wife than an Indian girl, Carson had said.

Suddenly the lurking pain struck again and Terry grabbed his head with a groan.

"What is it?" Willow-In-Storm asked in alarm. "Do you not feel well?"

He gritted his teeth. "I have this thing in my head. It started when I tried to bring back your sheep, and the horses ran over me."

"What thing do you mean?"

"They call it a tumor. It'll keep growing until it finally kills me."

"And when will that be?"

He sat up with frustration. "I don't know. . .soon." He looked at her face that seemed to glow in the moonlight peeking through the hogan's smoke hole. "That's why it wouldn't be fair to go back to your country and live with you. We would have so little time together."

She put a hand behind his head. "The only fair thing is to be with each other for as many days as the Holy Ones allow." She pulled him down to her smooth breasts. "Then we must enjoy every moment that is left."

CHAPTER FORTY-NINE

Another Long Walk began under the warm July sun, but this was a joyous one and the Navajos didn't care if their feet were bloodied during the journey, for they were going home. A train of fifty-six wagons, drawn by mules, carried the sick and feeble while the group of seven thousand tired but happy souls stretched out across the land for the journey west.

Terry O'Neill helped Standing Bear and Willow-In-Storm put their meager belongings together and they all went to join the others on the outskirts of Fort Sumner. Old Manuelito stood proudly at the head of the procession with a tired but happy expression on his bronze leathery face.

Terry was on his horse when the group began to move forward and he put down his hand.

"Come, Willow-In-Storm," he said, "you should ride with me. I don't want you walking."

She looked up with a brave smile and shook her head. "No, Teri-O-Neel. We have all walked together coming here, and we will all walk together going back."

He followed slowly on his horse as she went to join Standing Bear and Manuelito at the head of the line. Then the happy throng began walking with proud determination toward their sacred mountains and beautiful Dinetah that beckoned on the western horizon.

EPILOGUE

Following Kit Carson's military funeral at Fort Lyon in 1868, his body was taken by military escort to Boggsville, five miles away, and laid to rest beside his wife Josefa. Carson had requested that he and his wife be buried at Taos, New Mexico, however it was a year before their bodies were exhumed and taken over the Raton Pass, by wagon and team, to be reburied in the quaint cemetery at Taos. Their graves remained neglected until 1908 when the Masons, to which Kit had belonged, erected marble headstones.

Kit Carson's last-born child, Josefita, died at the age of 24 as Josephita Squire and was buried at Wagon Mound, New Mexico, then moved ten years later a few miles south to Las Vegas. It wasn't until 1991 that the grave was discovered to be that of Kit Carson's daughter; her body was moved to lie beside her parents in Taos.

The cemetery is now the Kit Carson Memorial Park and above Kit's grave, the American flag flies day and night to commemorate the year 1861, when Kit Carson, with patriotic fervor, nailed the flag to the Taos plaza pole.

The Kit Carson home, dating from 1843, is now a museum in Taos where visitors can see original artifacts and household utensils.

After Fort Sumner was deactivated, it was sold in 1870 to the famous landowner, Lucien B. Maxwell. In 1881 Fort Sumner became the site of another historical event when Billy The Kid was killed there by Sheriff Pat Garrett. The complex of buildings no longer exists, however the spot is now a State Monument.

General Carleton never ceased to feel proud of what he considered a major accomplishment at Bosque Redondo. He continued to serve in the Army until failing health forced him to retire. General James H. Carleton died of pneumonia on January 7, 1875.

After the Navajos returned to their beloved land, the ugly blemish of Bosque Redondo was erased by time and the desert winds. Over 200,000 Navajos still live on reservations in New Mexico, Arizona and Utah. Their generations have never forgotten the treacherous Long Walks and five years of imprisonment at the infamous Bosque Redondo reservation. It is a pivotal point from which Navajo time is measured.

THE END